THE LEGEND OF
THE CAPTAINS DAUGHTER

A Macey and Luke Quest

Jeff & Jacqi Lovell

A Mouse Gate Adventure

Mouse Gate Press
1103 Middlecreek
Friendswood, Texas 77546
281-992-3131 TEL
www.mousegate.com

Library of Congress Control Number: 2018933797

Printed in the United States of America with simultaneous printings in Australia, Canada, and United Kingdom.

FIRST EDITION
1 2 3 4 5 6 7 8 9 10

This book is dedicated to the memory of my grandparents, Wellborn and Marie Harrison.

At their home, I first found the book which fueled my imagination about pirates, *Doubloons* by Charles Driscoll.

They did their best to encourage a young writer and to pave the way for his dreams.

Award Winning Authors

Jeff and Jacqi Lovell are both natives of Chicago and former school teachers. Jeff has three degrees from the University of Illinois and a doctorate degree from Vanderbilt University. He taught writing and literature, and ran the drama program at two high schools. He has also served as a theater and film critic for a local TV station. Jacqi has a master's degree and has taught fourth through eighth grades, specializing in the fields of language arts and writing. She has also taught and facilitated Bible studies and parent education classes.

About the Book

Macey discovers her dad has taken a job across the country and must leave her home and friends. In order to soften the news, her parents take her on a vacation to Walt Disney World. At Blizzard Beach, she and a boy named Luke zoom down a water slide but pop up in water hundreds of miles away in the freezing Atlantic Ocean and a long way from shore. They are able to use a pendant that magically takes them to the shore of a secluded island. There a mysterious friend introduces them to the legend of the Ghost of White Island. The teens hear the courageous story of Martha Herring, forced into marriage with a brutal pirate, and abandoned on the miserable rock. The pirate goes back to sea, leaving Martha to guard his treasure. This is a recounting of her adventures and the challenges she and the people in her life endured. It is also the story of how the bonds of strong friendships can impact our lives.

PART 1

CHAPTER ONE

Macey Raines was in high spirits as she arrived home from school and sprinted through her front door. All of that enthusiasm was squashed within moments once her mom informed her of the dreadful news.

Thirteen years old, Macey was due to graduate from eighth grade at the end of the school year. Her mop of thick hair was braided at each side, swept back, and then tied at the back of her head with a fringed band to keep it out of her face as she walked home from school with her best friends. They all sported the uniform identifying their ages - jeans with small rips and tears up and down their legs, colorful Under Armor tees, lightweight hoodies, and high top black boots. They were all going to be high school freshman in the fall and Macey was looking forward with excitement to that new chapter in her life. The fact that the girls she had shared her deepest secrets with would be there alongside of her would make this transition even more special. As they walked, their conversation was filled with their anticipation of being in the same classes and the same sports next year.

That day had started out like most others. Macey went to her first class of the day, English with Mr. Schneider, where they were going to read *The Red Headed League*, a Sherlock Holmes short story by Sir Arthur Conan Doyle.

The class would be reading the story out loud in a Reader's theatre format, where the teacher read the narrative, but students in the class were assigned to play the parts of people in the play. The teacher asked her to read the part of the male character, red-headed Jabez Wilson. Even though it wasn't a girl's role and she certainly didn't fit the klutzy male character, her blaze of red hair made her a shoo-in for the part.

The class had a good laugh at that. Of course, they were not laughing at Macey, and she took it in stride even though she was already a little self-conscious about her hair color. She began to read in a halting manner.

"Macey," said her teacher, sensing her discomfort, "If you don't want to read the part, you don't have to. I thought of you because I've heard you imitating a British cockney accent and I think you could get into the character."

"Yes, sir," she mumbled.

"Do you want me to ask someone else?" asked the teacher.

"No, Mr. Schneider," she said. "I can do it."

Her teacher's comments gave her the confidence she needed to gain control and in a few moments, she was able to concentrate on her cockney accent, which the rest of the class enjoyed a great deal. She soon found herself having fun with the assignment.

Later that morning she had a study hall in the library. She finished her math homework and saw that her friends were still busy with their assignments. Glancing around, she noticed an old book called *Doubloons* resting on the other end of the table. She picked it up and saw it was printed in 1938, written by a man named Charles Driscoll, and subtitled 'The Story of Buried Treasure.' Her tablemates were still studying so she skimmed over the first chapter of the book.

At first, she was puzzled at who would have left a rather valuable book on the table, but decided it looked interesting and began reading.

Soon she was learning about the age of Piracy in precolonial America, which took place from 1715 through about 1725. The chapter dealt with the story of Blackbeard, perhaps the most vicious of the violent, murdering brigands of those years.

Next, she read about another pirate from that era, a violent thug named Sandy Gordon who led a mutiny against Captain John Herring, the master of the war sloop *Porpoise*. Captain Herring, for some reason not recorded in history, brought his daughter with him on the ship. Once he took over the ship, Gordon murdered the former captain while his terrified daughter looked on.

On orders from Gordon, the pirates pitched Captain Herring over the side into the North Atlantic. Then Gordon turned his attention to the Captain's daughter, fourteen-year-old Martha, who was forced to marry the scoundrel who had murdered her father. To make matters worse, he then locked her in a dismal cabin in the lower decks of the ship. She was allowed out of the cabin only when the ship was too far from any shore to escape.

After a while, Gordon abandoned his young wife on a gloomy, dismal island about ten miles out in the frigid Atlantic from Portsmouth, New Hampshire. She was several months pregnant by then, and Gordon had his men construct a one-room cabin for her to live in while he was away at sea. He wanted to make sure no one would be able to find her.

He left her a few weapons to defend herself: a brace of pistols, a cutlass and a dagger. She didn't know how to use them, but she kept them near.

The cabin, constructed from rocks scattered around the island, was drafty and cold, and Martha was bitterly lonely. Gordon had his men bring several chests of treasure ashore and they hid them in the cabin.

Macy, reading this chapter of early American folklore, realized that Martha was only a year older than she when all of this occurred. She shuddered at the thought of going through everything this young girl had endured. Macey found herself trying to imagine how she would have survived if she had been in Martha's place.

Macey leaned back in her library chair, staring at the book. The story of Martha troubled her since there was no satisfactory ending to the story. No information was given about what happened to her after Gordon died.

So, when she arrived home Macey told her mom about English class where she had been embarrassed about her reading and how she had been selected because of her red hair. Then she told her about the book she had found in the library and shared the legend of Martha with her mother, who listened and hugged her daughter. Mom assured her that a ship from Britain or the American Colonies would have found Martha and brought her to the mainland. Her words didn't comfort her daughter much.

When Macey finished telling her mom all about her day, Mom got up, made them both some hot cocoa, and invited her to sit down with her at the kitchen table.

"Macey," she began, "I have some exciting news to share with you. Your dad received a wonderful job opportunity."

"Wow, that's great. Mom. When does he start?"

"Well, honey," said Mom, "it really is good news, but I have to tell you something and I don't want you to get upset. I want you to just listen and we can talk about whatever questions you might have."

"What are you talking about? What do you mean? Why would I be upset?" Her mother's tone was beginning to cause her concern.

"Well," Mom began slowly, trying to choose her words carefully, "this new job requires that we move so you would be starting in a new school in the fall."

"What do you mean, move? Move where?" asked Macey cautiously.

Mom tried not to stumble giving her reply, "I am afraid we will be leaving California and moving to a suburb of Chicago as soon as school is out for the summer."

"What!? You can't do that to me. Not now. Not when I am going to just start high school. Not when all my friends are here. How am I supposed to make new friends? I hate Chicago. I hate cold weather. I hate that you are making me do this." And Macey stormed off to her room.

Mom sighed and busied herself cleaning up the kitchen, wishing she could make this news more appealing to her daughter. She understood it would be difficult for her to move and start over, but she wished she could help Macey see it as an adventure.

As Macey left for school the next morning she dreaded having to tell her friends the news. She just wished this year would go on and on, never ending. If she started talking, she was afraid she would just break down and cry, and what good would that do?

As Macey sauntered through the door that afternoon, Mom again had hot cocoa waiting for her and motioned for her to have a seat.

"You know," Mom said, "this is a scary time for all of us, not just you. I am just as worried about making new friends as you are. I wish we could stay here, too, but..."

"Why don't you just tell that to Dad? Tell him we don't want to move. Tell him this is a bad decision," cried Macey.

"Because we are a family, and we support each other, and this is the job your dad has always dreamed of. I want the best for him and I love him so I am not going to make him feel guilty about this. I have to trust this will work out to be a good thing for us all."

"I want to believe that, too, Mom. I really do, but it's just hard. How am I going to manage a new school where I have no friends? I love it here. I have lived here my whole life."

Mom pulled her closer and gave her a hug. "It will work out, you'll see, honey."

"I hope so, Mom, I hope so," Macey replied as she pulled away and trudged up the stairs to her room.

The school year came to a close and that last day Macey said her tearful good-byes to her teachers and some of the kids. Her best friends had already had a going away party for her the previous week and she avoided them that last afternoon. She just couldn't handle the emotional response it would generate. As she arrived home she was feeling sorry for herself.

The moving truck arrived the next morning. Dad had already left for their house in Geneva, IL to start his new job. As the packing crew received their final instructions from Mom, Macey walked out the double doors to their patio one last time.

She wiped the tears from her eyes as she gazed around at all the trees and flowers that made their yard so pretty. Glancing at the pool reminded her of all the pool parties they had hosted for friends and family since she was a little girl. Her mom taught her, and many of her friends, how to swim in that pool. She would have no pool in Illinois. Her eyes wandered over to the bush where they had held a little ceremony and buried her guinea pig when she was six. She wanted the memory of this whole scene to be imprinted in her mind forever.

Their new home was nice and Macey loved her spacious new bedroom, but it wasn't California. She still hadn't really met anyone four weeks after the move. She spent a lot of time on their deck, reading and trying to keep in touch with her old friends, but she felt those relationships slipping away ever so slightly since her move.

"Macey, why don't you go for a bike ride or head over to the new school to see about signing up for one of the sport camps," suggested Mom, who was getting concerned about her lack of interest to become involved in anything regarding her new school for the fall.

When her dad came home that evening, he and Mom went out for a walk together. "I am wondering what to do about Macey," she shared. "I am worried about her unwillingness to try to adjust to the move."

"Well," said Dad, "I may have something that will help," his eyes twinkling. "My boss wants me to go to Orlando to entertain some clients and he said I could take the family..."

"Oh, Jim," interrupted Mom, "it might be just the thing to snap her out of this attitude. That is her favorite place in the whole world and we haven't been able to go for awhile."

"Just what I was thinking," he agreed.

They decided to make this a surprise trip for Macey so Mom did her packing after she was in bed or early in the morning, whenever she could sneak something into suitcases hidden in her closet. Dad took care of all the travel arrangements and reservations through his office and their trip was set for the next week-end.

Saturday arrived and Macey was awakened by her mom opening her door at 5:30 am and announcing, "Macey! Time to rise and shine, and we leave in half an hour!"

Macey tumbled out of bed, looked at her clock, and then thought her mom had lost her mind. "What are you talking about? Mom, have you lost it? Look at the time? What do you mean we are leaving in a half hour?"

"Oh, well, sorry, I thought you might be interested in coming to Disney World with us. But if you would rather go back to sleep...". Mom did not get to finish the sentence.

Macey set a personal record for showering and getting dressed, and the limo driver pulled into their driveway a few minutes later. He drove them to O'Hare Airport, Chicago's gigantic aviation hub.

On the plane, Macey plied her parents with question after question: "Where are we staying again? What's it like? Is there a pool?"

Mom, as excited as her daughter, explained, "We are staying on the Disney property, a place called Port Orleans French Quarter. Our room looks out on the waterway, not far from the boat dock. You can hop on a boat and go straight to Disney Springs. The French Quarter has a great food court. As a matter of fact, I am looking forward to my first beignet, those spectacular doughnuts they make on site drenched in powdered sugar. But there is also a terrific pool area, and my favorite, a great hot tub." Macey smiled at her mom's description.

Four hours later, they landed in Orlando. They followed the signs to catch the Magical Express Bus to Walt Disney World, and their resort. To Macey's surprise, they didn't even have to pick up their luggage. "Come on, Macey," grinned Dad. "Disney will pick up our luggage and take it right to our room for us."

Nor did they have to wait long before boarding their bus and setting off for the resort. The bus even had entertainment: a couple of classic Disney cartoons and a Disney trivia quiz, which they passed with flying colors. Unseen by Macey, Mom gave Dad a little lift of her eyebrow, indicating pleasure that their daughter was actually laughing again. He smiled in return.

Two hours after that, they had settled into their room at the The French Quarter. After some brief unpacking, the family went their various ways. Daddy went to the Magnolia Golf Course, where he was going to meet some clients for a sales/golf/dinner extravaganza. That, Mom explained, was why they were able to come to Florida: Dad was going to entertain clients.

Typical, thought Macey. Business always came first for Dad. She and Mom probably wouldn't see a whole lot of him. Macey felt bad at first that Daddy wasn't able to be with them every day, but she loved Disney and there was so much to do that she figured she and Mom would be fine on their own for most of the time. Besides, he would join them a few times during their stay.

They decided to start their visit to EPCOT with a visit to the

American Pavilion, located opposite the main entrance. As they walked through Future World they decided to take the launch across the lake. Arriving at the American Experience pavilion, they noticed that it was not too crowded and the show was due to start in a few moments.

The show began in a rotunda inside the main entrance. An adult vocal group came out and entertained the assembled audience with arrangements of American folk and popular songs. They were dressed in period costumes and sang in perfect harmony, with no musical accompaniment. All must have been impressed with their performance because the crowd rewarded the singers with a standing ovation and a rousing round of applause.

When the songs were over, the visitors left to go into the auditorium for the presentation. Macey took the opportunity to speak to one of the singers. The woman had remained a few minutes at the end of the concert and Macey noticed that she was quite tall, maybe even a little intimidating, as she approached her.

"That was fantastic," Macey raved. "I was in choir in school, and hope to be in the performance choir once I get in high school next year. You guys were wonderful." As they spoke, Macey had a hard time trying not to stare at the woman's eyes. They were unusually light and almost golden in color.

"Thank you," the singer said, delighted by the greeting from an enthusiastic teenager. "Why don't you and your mom meet me after the movie presentation? I'd enjoy showing you some of our backstage and a few additional exhibits."

"Thank you," said Mom. "We'd be honored to take advantage of your gracious offer." The singer smiled and told them where she would meet them.

The presentation was very moving and filled Macey and her mom with pride in their American heritage. In particular the Civil War story and its songs, such as *Two Brothers*, touched her deeply:

Two brothers on their way, Two brothers on their way.   One wore blue and one wore gray, As they marched along their way. The fife and the drum began to play, All on a beautiful morning.

The saddest of the American wars affected Mom, a southerner by birth, and she and Macey had tears in their eyes as she watched the movie.

As they left the auditorium, they found the singer who had been kind to them. She had removed her hat and her long, almost white, hair trailed down her back. She shook hands with them and introduced herself as Mara. Mom asked, "So where are you from, Mara?"

Mara responded rather mysteriously, "Oh, many places," and quickly changed the subject.

The tour lasted about an hour, and the remarkable Disney Animatronic characters of Benjamin Franklin and Mark Twain were worth visiting in themselves.

After finishing their tour, Mara took them to outside to a Disney snack kiosk where they enjoyed ice cream bars in the shape of the Mickey Mouse logo.

"Have you taken any American History, Macey?" asked Mara.

"This is a great place to learn about the history, isn't it?" Mom smiled at Macey. "Tell Mara what you've been reading, Macey," she said, embracing her daughter's shoulders.

Macey went into a brief description about her discovery of

the book, *Doubloons,* and the pirates who terrorized the east coast. Mara's eyes twinkled as she listened with some curiosity.

"We don't do a lot with the early colonies here in the pavilion," Mara explained. "It's too bad. A lot of American history gets left out." She looked at her watch. "I have really enjoyed chatting with you, but I am afraid I have to leave and get ready for our next performance. It was so nice meeting you both and I hope you have a magical day here in Disney."

"Thank you, Mara," said Macey.

Mara turned to leave, but then abruptly stopped, pivoted around and said, "Here, Macey, I want to give you something very unique and valuable. I'm afraid it has gone dark for the moment. But when it is time to use it, it will glow for you." Then she handed Macey a beautiful glass-like clear pendant on a gold chain.

"What do you mean, gone dark?" asked Macey. "How do you use it? You hardly know me, are you sure you want to give it to me?"

"You hold the pendant up in front of you," explained Mara. "You'll understand the first time you are called to use it. Don't worry. I think you will find it to be a very special pendant. I know you are meant to have it."

Mom and Macey exchanged quizzical glances with one another.

"It's certainly beautiful," Mom said. "What an amazing necklace." She held it up to the sun, but nothing happened.

Mara added, "Keep it around your neck. It won't leave you, I promise." She smiled, and then walked off and disappeared through the cast doors.

Mom and Macey puzzled over those words. "What do you

think she meant that I was supposed to have this? And I will know how to use it?" asked Macey.

"I don't have a clue," answered Mom. "She certainly was mysterious, don't you agree?"

Macey nodded. "At any rate, it is quite pretty and I would just enjoy wearing it," added Mom.

By this time, they were both hungry so decided to catch an early dinner close by at Restaurant Marrakesh in Moroccan Pavilion. They only had to wait a few minutes before being seated since they arrived at an off-hour.

"Wow, this is really unusual food," announced Macey, sounding unsure about their decision to eat here.

"I thought it might be nice for us to be a little adventurous. You know, try things we have never had before," laughed Mom. "Besides, I hear they have very interesting entertainment while you eat. I think I will get the shish kabob. What about you?"

"I think I will order the lemon chicken," said Macey, playing it safe.

The waiter returned and they gave him their order.

While waiting they each had one of the special Berber Passion drinks and continued their discussion about the strange woman who gave Macey the unusual pendant.

As they began eating their dinner, an exotic looking woman with long, dark hair stepped onto the open area. She wore a scanty, purple, hip-hugging costume made of filmy material with lots of embroidered jewels and began dancing to the Turkish music, which had an almost hypnotizing quality to it. Macey's mouth fell open as she watched the woman wriggle her way around the floor. She didn't know people could move their hips, let alone their whole bodies, in so many directions so quickly. Not only that, but the whole time she was dancing she was also clanging little cymbals attached to her fingers. It was all very mesmerizing to Macey.

Mom had to restrain from laughing out loud. "I told you they had an unusual show here. Welcome to your first belly dancer show. Maybe you could get a summer job here," teased Mom.

Macey just rolled her eyes and jabbed at her mom's arm. "Oh, yeah, I'm all over that!"

They finished dinner, split the mouth-watering pastry dessert called Bastille for Two, and then decided to hop back on the launch to cross the lake and check out some of the Future World rides.

The theme song at *Journey into Imagination* left Macey singing the song for the rest of the evening.

"Ok, now we have to go over to *Test Track.*" announced Macey.

"I don't know. That is a really fast ride, isn't it?" asked Mom. "Oh, well, might as well live dangerously. Let's do it."

The ride allowed them to design their own cars and compete against everyone else's designs. As they left the ride they discovered that Mom's car was the overall winner.

Then they walked over to the Universe of Energy where they laughed at the Ellen DeGeneres and Jamie Lee Curtis pre-show comedy routine. "I always love to see the Animatronic dinosaurs as we travel through this ride. They do such a great job making them so realistic," commented Mom as they exited the pavilion. "Are you ready to head back to the resort?"

"Can we just hit *Spaceship Earth* before we leave? Please?" begged Macey.

"Sure," agreed Mom. "It's on the way out." So, they wound their way through the huge ball in their little car, enjoying the familiar scenes of history presented in the calm ride.

The two were desperately tired by the time they returned their room at the French Quarter. Macey was in a deep, sound sleep by the time her father returned.

The family planned to fill their days with visits to the Animal Kingdom and Hollywood Studios, and spent two days at the Magic Kingdom and added another trip to Epcot.

Macey would remember this as the best vacation she ever took with her parents. She wore the Pendant faithfully every day, including to the swimming pools. She couldn't see, of course, that her whole life was about to change.

*****

The next day Dad headed for a very early tee time at the Palm golf course. Mom and Macey made plans to meet him at Blizzard Beach. They agreed to take advantage of the warm weather and all the fun activities at the water park. The girls changed into their swimwear, stopped for a quick breakfast, and hopped on the bus to the water park. Mom decided to camp out in the shade under a tree on a lounge with a good book while Macey took off to investigate all the different water rides and attractions. She met a few teens from Canada, another from Georgia, and another from St. Lucia in the Caribbean. They played some card games, swam in the pools, and finally talked Macey into going down one of the huge water slides. She went down three times, giggling and laughing.

"Okay," said one of the kids, "Let's see how you do with Summit Plummet."

Before agreeing to get in line, Macey checked the guidebook for a description of the water ride. She read about what the authors called "The Park's Finest...and Most Fearsome." Macey then took a good look at the drop, billed as 120 feet, and sheer.

"Yow," she said to one of the other kids.

"Yeah, I know," he said, grinning. "Not only that, but you can't see where you're going. They have a timer, too, so you can see how fast you're going—"

"Oh shut it, Tim," said one of the other kids. "You're making her nervous." Macey giggled a little, and then nodded to her new friends.

"Okay," she managed. "I can do this." She reached up and grasped the crystal around her neck. To her surprise, all doubts and nervousness vanished.

When her turn came, she launched herself, crossed her arms over her chest and tried to keep her eyes open. She felt like she'd fallen off a cliff and the scream she gave echoed around the area. Then she was down, through the tunnel, and rocketing into space.

She hit the pool, and felt a strange mixture of terror and laughter.

She began to swim in the water, a bit awkwardly, and sank a bit. In the next few moments, though, she fought her way to the surface –

And screamed with terror.

She looked around, treading water and pivoting in circles. There was no slide, no Blizzard Beach Park, no music. Worst of all, she was alone in a vast expanse of water.

Now she realized that she was in saltwater. Last year, she'd gone on vacation to the beach with Mom and Dad near Duck,

North Carolina, swimming in the salty ocean with a beach and hanging out with special friends. That meant that somehow, she'd been transported to an ocean.

But which ocean? Where?

She became aware that she was shivering. This wasn't the ocean near Duck. The air was warm, perhaps mid-70s, with a gentle breeze, but the water was cold. She noticed there was a coastline and small beach about 200 yards away.

Macey fought down the panic. She tried to think through the situation, but had no idea. "Mom?" she yelled. Of course, there was no answer. She didn't really expect one but now she was truly frightened.

"Oh, boy," she thought. She continued to tread water—

And then something happened. The water erupted a few feet from her, and again she let out a little scream as a boy about her age rose up from the water.

A few moments went by as he too pivoted, looking in all directions. He had shaggy blonde hair and startling green eyes. He shook his long hair and began to tread water.

"What in the world? Where are we?" he screeched, and she could hear his voice tremble slightly.

"I know it's the ocean," she said. "But this isn't Blizzard Beach."

"Blizzard Beach?" he asked, puzzled.

"Yeah, at Disney World," she said. "All I know is that I went down the slide at Blizzard Beach called *Summit Plummet*—"

"Disney World?" he asked. "You were at Disney World?"

"Well, yeah," she said. "How about you?"

"Well, me too! I went down that slide as well. I hit the water, came up, and here I am."

"Okay," she shivered. "Nice to meet you. Meanwhile, I'm freezing."

"You have a pendant too," he exclaimed, and held up his necklace, which was identical to hers. "Oh, by the way, I'm Luke Grant. I suggest we swim toward that shore and get out of this freezing water."

"Yes, I agree, let's get moving. I'm Macey Racine. I hope we can swim that far. We can try to figure this out once we get ashore." At that moment she lifted her pendant, holding it tightly so it would not drift off her neck.

"Look," Luke exclaimed, pointing at her pendant and lifting his up as well. "The circle inside the pendant is expanding." Their eyes widened in both surprise and excitement.

"Quick, let's swim through it," Macey shouted. He nodded his agreement. They grabbed onto each other and in the next moment they found themselves in a couple of feet of much warmer water. The very beach they had spotted while bobbing in the ocean was just steps away.

Still holding hands, they walked forward and stepped on to a warm beach, with warm white sand. At once they became much more comfortable. They plopped down on a log and tried to make sense of what had just happened.

"That was scary," said Macey.

"Yea," agreed Luke. "But a lot more exciting then the rides at Blizzard Beach. And it turned out o.k. I mean we are not hurt or anything."

Macey just gave him one of her exasperated looks. She was about to give him a curt reply when she looked up and saw that a tall, lean woman with bright, almost white, hair hanging straight down stood in front of them. She smiled and handed them each a towel. "Mara!" stammered Macey. "How did you get here?"

"You mean you know her?" asked Luke.

Macey introduced Luke to Mara and explained how they knew each other. Then she said, "We don't know what happened? We went down some of the park slides and we wound up in the ocean!"

Mara just gave a little smirk. "Well, I can't tell you for sure, but my guess is that the pendants took you to the North Atlantic, and you landed here, near White Island."

"White Island?" asked Luke.

"That is the Island where the pirate Sandy Gordon abandoned his young wife, isn't it?" asked Macey, excited to be able to explain. "I just finished reading all about her story in the library at school."

"Who? What story are you talking about?" questioned Luke.

"Well, it's quite a mystery," said Mara. "It'll take some time to relate the entire story of the Treasure of White Island."

"There's a treasure?" asked Macey, and she and Luke exchanged glances.

"Yes," said Mara. "Come on, let's sit in the sun and I'll tell you about it."

Mara led them to a beach fire, which was burning warmly. A small barbeque grill stood next to the fire, and the coals were hot and ready for grilling. She gave them each a fleece warm-up suit, which they slipped on with some speed. The sun felt warm as they sat and relaxed on a couple of beach chairs.

"I'm going to tell you a ghost story about this island," said Mara. "Don't be afraid, you are perfectly safe here. Why don't you grill a couple of those hot dogs? I imagine you're a little hungry."

"A ghost story. Cool!" said Luke.

They put a couple of hot dogs on the small grille. While Luke attended to that chore, Mara laid out some buns, a bag of chips, and produced some plastic dinnerware and a couple of plates. She reached into a small cooler and handed them each a can of soda, root beer for Macey and orange for Luke. "You can have more soda if you want," she said.

The teens were eager to join in at the sight of food. They were both ravenous by now, but also confused by everything that had happened. "How did you know my favorite soda was orange?" asked Luke.

"And that I loved root beer," added Macey.

Luke persisted, "And what about all this food, and the grill? Where did they come from? This island is so small and it looks deserted. How did you get here if Macey saw you in Walt Disney World?"

Mara just grinned and avoided answering. Instead she said, "Macey, while we eat why don't you tell Luke what you know about Gordon, his young wife Martha, and this island from your book in the library."

"Oh, I would love to." Macey then related some of the history of Martha, her pirate husband, his mutiny, and the capture of her father's ship.

The two teenagers were enjoying their beach party with this strange new friend, but soon they realized how far away they were from their families and Disney World.

"Mara," said Macey, "this is really nice and all but I think our parents are going to be worried about us. Do you have any idea how we get back or let them know we are ok?" Luke glanced at

Mara to hear the answer to the question he had wanted to ask as well.

Mara looked them straight in the eye and responded, "I can assure both of you that time is not quite the same when you are with me, and I promise you will return to the exact time in the water parks at Walt Disney World as when you left when our time together has ended. Now, would you like to hear about the adventure and mystery that surrounds this island?"

"Definitely!" they replied.

CHAPTER TWO

Martha and Owen

Mara began, "I must begin the story with a bit of a warning, dear young friends." Don't go to White Island on a moonlit night, especially if you are afraid of ghosts.

This island rises with several other rocky islands above the North Atlantic, about ten miles out from Portsmouth, New Hampshire. Like the other rocks in the Isle of Shoals chain, White Island is cold and rocky, wind-swept and inhospitable much of the year.

A famous treasure, according to legend, lies hidden on the rock. But White Island is the subject of another, even more famous legend. A ghost story! The ghost of a young woman named Martha Herring walks here.

It was about 300 years ago when mutineers took over Captain John Herring's ship.

"You will hang for this, Gordon," spat Herring before he died.

It was after Gordon turned *Porpoise* into a pirate ship renamed *The Flying Scott* that he met up with Blackbeard. Not long after that fateful alliance Gordon abandoned Martha here on White Island. He sailed away and threatened her life if she didn't promise to protect his treasure. She stood on the southeast side of the island and watched as her husband's ship disappeared over the horizon.

Gordon and his crew met his match within a couple of days. He attacked a small and defenseless passenger ship, intending to fill his treasure chests with more booty. However, in the midst of his attack, a British warship named H. M. S. *Renown* set upon Gordon.

The vastly superior British man of war defeated Gordon's ship. The pirate crew, pleading and begging for mercy, received speedy trials. With few exceptions, the pirates were hanged and thrown over the side to their watery grave. Gordon never returned to his pregnant young wife, now alone on an island rock in the merciless Atlantic Ocean.

Even though her bones have lain in a grave on a neighboring island for 300 years, Martha's ghost has been sighted on walks in the moonlight at a low spot on the island. She is always seen dressed in the garb of a female pirate.

People who have spotted her ghost say that she stands on that corner where her husband's ship was last seen, staring out to sea. She doesn't see them, but speaks in a soft, but audible voice. Over and over, she says, *He will return. He will return.*

Guests at the Retreat Center on nearby Star Island, the largest of the rocks in the Isle of Shoals chain, laugh when they hear the legend of the Ghost of White Island. They wonder, who would believe such a foolish story? A ghost? Pirates? Absurd.

However, often they end up bidding goodbye to others who are leaving for the mainland by repeating—in some cases laughing and mocking—the young woman's cry of loneliness: *You will return. You will return.*

At this point Mara paused to tell the teens, "Now that you have both heard the background about Martha, let me share the story of another girl about your age, Macey, and her experience with White Island." By now, both Luke and Macey were wide eyed and had pretty much forgotten about eating.

*****

A teenager named McKenna met the Ghost of White Island when grief had all but overwhelmed her.

McKenna's life fell apart one afternoon in January. The first semester of McKenna's freshman year in high school had just ended. The bus ride home from school after her last final exam found her giggling at everything her friends said.

As she left the school at 11:00 A.M., she buttoned up her winter coat. The sun shone bright and the temperature hovered in the mid-40s. Though warm for January in the northern suburbs of Chicago, the weather that day didn't fool her. McKenna saw the storm clouds in the west. A big midwinter storm would hit the area soon. Thunder and lightning and drenching sleet would drive all activities indoors.

McKenna told her friends that she intended to go out to lunch with her mom, who had offered a celebration for McKenna's outstanding first semester in high school. Dad had gone out of town to Puerto Rico, entertaining some clients with four days of golf.

She walked up the long driveway to the house, listening to the sound of some winter birds in the large trees on their property. She was pondering how to spend a few days off from school, appreciating the break from the stress of studying for exams. She noticed a flash of bright red and smiled to think about the cardinals that frequently ate at their wild bird feeder.

The day fell apart once she walked in the front door, singing a greeting. Mom sat on the large leather couch in the living room. She rose as McKenna came in. "Honey," she said, her eyes filled with worry.

Mom wasn't crying but as soon as McKenna saw her

mother, she knew that something big had happened. Her stomach fell!

"What is it?" McKenna asked, not sure she really wanted an answer. Mom motioned for her to take a seat next to her. McKenna slid into the sofa and Mom put a loving arm around her.

"Honey," Mom said, but then didn't speak for a few moments. "I just received a call from Mr. Denton," she said.

"Didn't he go with Daddy to Puerto Rico?"

"Yes, he did. He called me from the hotel in San Juan."

"Why would he call you? He isn't even—" McKenna stopped and looked at her mom. "Daddy. Something's happened to Daddy—He's gone?" she screeched, her hands grasping Mom. Mom hesitated. McKenna knew.

Mom told her that her father, Alan DiBiasi, died that morning of a heart attack on the golf course in Puerto Rico while entertaining his clients. McKenna's world seemed to collapse as Mom sketched in the details. The girl could not stop crying.

As she came down the steps a few mornings later, she saw Mom standing by the front door. Through the picture window, she saw a FedEx truck pulling down the long driveway.

"Did we just have something delivered?" she asked, still numb to everything around her. Mom pointed to several boxes on the porch. Together, they brought them in. The hotel in Puerto Rico had sent Dad's suitcase, golf clubs, and personal items.

A smaller package, wrapped in brown paper, sat on the porch by the front door. "What about this one?" asked McKenna, pointing. She lifted it but it was heavier than the others.

Mom put her arms around her daughter and pulled the girl's head against her shoulder. "Honey," said Mom. "The San Juan funeral home sent your father's ashes to us."

McKenna tried to be brave. "Oh Mommy," she whispered, dropping the package as she backed away, horrified. Then the tears fell again. Mom stood embracing her daughter while McKenna wept with grief.

"What shall we do with the ashes?" she asked in her gentle North Carolina accent.

McKenna thought for a few moments. She had to swallow and make an effort to say, "Door County." Mom nodded.

Mother and daughter packed up Dad's car, a shiny, sleek black BMW convertible. McKenna had always enjoyed the rich smell of the leather upholstery and the feel of the breeze in her hair when riding with her dad. Today, though, they drove in silence across the Wisconsin border, then through Milwaukee on their way to Door County.

They pulled into the driveway of their summer home just before the glacial winter darkness covered the beach. The weather was bitter cold with a howling west wind. The steel gray waves on Lake Michigan boomed on the shore, hurling an icy spray into the air.

"Can you go through with this?" asked Mom before they started down the path.

"Yes," McKenna asserted. "Let's do it."

McKenna and her mom, Anna, walked together to the beach, their hair whipping around their faces. They opened the package and scattered the ashes on the shore of Lake Michigan. The powerful west wind blew the ashes out onto the lake where they vanished from sight.

Mother and daughter hugged while McKenna wept her goodbye to her father. Anna took her to dinner even though McKenna insisted she wasn't hungry. Some barbequed chicken and a baked potato raised her spirits. She and Mom split a piece of Door County cherry pie, sharing memories of happier times at their vacation home.

As they were driving home McKenna turned to her mother. "You aren't as upset by Daddy's death as I am," she said, matter-of-factly. The statement sounded like an accusation, harsher and nastier than she intended. She decided not to apologize, though.

Mom gave a little nod, not responding to the bitter tone in her daughter's voice. She didn't answer for several moments.

Mom's reaction confirmed McKenna's impression of the marriage her parents had lived with for eighteen years. As she got older, McKenna thought her parents were no longer in love, even though they stayed together. For example, Mom still went by her maiden name, Anna O'Neill.

Mom, though, didn't rise to the fight. She stared down the interstate. She took her left hand off the steering wheel and ran her fingers through her long copper-colored hair.

When Mom finally spoke, she chose her words with care, "I know you're heartbroken. I'd like to keep you out of school for a few extra days and take you to the ocean."

McKenna was bewildered. "To the ocean?"

"Yes," said Mom. "Remember, I grew up in North Carolina, not far from the Atlantic. I always went to the shore when I was sad. When my parents died, I drove over to the ocean. I'd watch the waves, and listen to the wind and the calls of the gulls. Being there, listening to the rhythm of the sea, breathing in the fresh salt air. It always restored my spirits."

"You want to go to North Carolina?" said McKenna, surprised.

"No, not North Carolina," said Mom. "I thought we might drive to New York and follow the coast to Maine. Say, Bar Harbor." McKenna thought about her mother's suggestion. Mom reached across the seat and stroked her daughter's hair, which so resembled her own. Her mother's gentle hands had always comforted her.

McKenna shrugged, but felt more excited than she allowed herself to show. A trip like this with Mom might be wonderful. "Okay," she said.

They decided to have a memorial service for Daddy in a couple of weeks, and left the next day. Mom took back roads to let her daughter see the beautiful scenery across Indiana and Ohio. They stayed overnight in a bed-and-breakfast in the Amish country of southeast Pennsylvania. They reached the coast the next day and drove up to Boston. Late on the third afternoon, Mom stopped for the night at a hotel in Portsmouth, New Hampshire.

As they carried their overnight bags to their room,

Mom said, "Are you too tired for an ocean expedition after supper?"

McKenna smiled, and then giggled. "No, that sounds great."

"Look," said Mom, holding out a brochure. We can go with a local company to Isle of Shoals."

"What's that?"

Mom read the folder. "It's a chain of islands about ten miles out from Portsmouth. It's going to be a beautiful night, with a full moon."

McKenna grinned and nodded, excited about a trip on the open ocean. Mom called the charter company.

Mom and McKenna, bundled up against the cold, were the only passengers that evening on a cabin cruiser with Sue McCarty, a longtime resident of the coastal town. The full moon illuminated the calm ocean.

Though McKenna's heart brimmed with grief she loved the trip across the ten miles of open ocean. Despite the chill, she stood outside for several minutes, the wind whipping her hair. The spray felt wonderful and she breathed deep, embracing the peacefulness that the ocean can bring to the heart. She went back into the cabin, where Mom hugged her and smiled as the boat knifed through the gentle swells.

Sue took them first to the largest island, Star Island, and then to a couple of the others. As she piloted the boat, she told them stories of the islands, some of which belong to the state of Maine while the rest belong to New Hampshire. "Tell you what," said Sue. "Before we head back, let's go over to White Island. We'll look at the lighthouse and walk around the island. Maybe we'll meet Martha."

"Who?" asked McKenna.

"A legend," said Sue, with a mischievous grin. The reply took McKenna aback and she and Mom exchanged puzzled glances. Mom looked amused.

Sue anchored the boat in shallow water on the east side of White Island, and lowered a small rubber raft. They rowed to a small beach and clambered ashore.

Sue illuminated a path with a powerful flashlight as they scrabbled together to the top of the island. She pointed to the land bridge on the northern side. "That connects White Island to

Seavey Island when the tide is low." Over there—'' she pointed to a small rocky island to the northeast—"is Sugar Island."

"I'm going to explore," said McKenna, anxious to walk about on her own. Mom and Sue agreed, and she sauntered off.

McKenna found a spot on the southeast side of the island and sat, staring out at the sea. She listened to the boom of the waves as they crashed on the rocks of the island. The moon was high in the sky, burning the island with a ghostly white light.

However, she did feel a peace descend on her, as Mom had said it would. She licked her lips, enjoying the salt taste from the ocean spray that dampened her face. Then she remembered.

Oh Daddy, why did you have to die?

McKenna let go and sobbed with her grief at the first death she'd ever experienced. As her tears fell, she fumbled in her jeans for a handkerchief. As she pulled it out of her pocket, a quarter fell out and rolled away. McKenna followed the coin, which came to rest behind a rock beside the path. She knelt and moved the rock a little—

And stared in surprise.

Her quarter lay on top of a shiny object, about an inch in diameter. McKenna picked it up. Even in the moonlight, she could see that she held a gold coin.

She couldn't make out the markings well. Still she knew it had to be valuable—

"He will return," said a whispery voice behind her.

Startled, McKenna gave a little scream and leapt to her feet. She turned to see a girl about her own age walking down the path toward her. "He will return," the girl said again. McKenna saw that the moonlight created an aura around the girl.

"That has to be Martha, right," squealed Macey. Mara smiled and

continued.

The girl, slim, about five feet tall, wore a long costume like a pirate might wear against the cold of the evening. McKenna stared at the girl's striking hair, which blew about her head. It looked a great deal like McKenna's own hair. The costume made her think that she was looking at a pirate.

The girl reached up and tucked her hair behind her ear. She then strolled down the path, slow and unhurried. "I'm sorry I screamed. You startled me," said McKenna when her heart slowed a little. She managed a smile. "I didn't think anyone else was here on the island—"

But the girl didn't respond. She walked past McKenna and stared out to sea, looking to the southeast. Again, she repeated, "He will return."

McKenna walked toward the girl. "Are you deaf?" she asked, concern in her voice. When the girl didn't respond, McKenna reached out to tap her shoulder.

Her hand touched nothing. It went right through the girl.

McKenna's stomach lurched in fear. She shivered, near panic with eerie dread.

She turned and ran up the path to the top of the island. "Mom!" she yelled as she ran.

Anna, perhaps twenty yards away, turned at the note of terror in her daughter's voice. She rushed to her daughter, followed by Sue. "What is it?" asked Mom, her soothing voice calming McKenna.

"A girl," said McKenna, pointing. "A pirate girl. But she's— she's not there."

Sue turned and hurried to the top of the path. "No one is here, McKenna. It's all right."

Mom and McKenna joined Sue and looked down. Sue was right. The girl was nowhere to be seen. "What the—" said McKenna. She pointed, astonished. "She was standing right there."

"Did the girl say something?" asked Sue.

"Yes," said McKenna. "Twice she said, '*he will return.*'"

Sue broke into a broad grin. "Congratulations," she said. "You've just met the most famous inhabitant of the island. I'm sorry she scared you."

"What?" said McKenna.

"Oh, yes. You've met the Ghost of White Island. Her name is—or was—Martha Herring."

McKenna, her heart still pounding, didn't know what to say. Looking down, she realized that she was still clutching her handkerchief and the two coins. "Oh!" she said. She held the gold coin out to Sue.

Sue shone a flashlight on it. "Where did you find this?"

McKenna pointed out the rock on the path where she'd found the coin. "Is it valuable?" she asked.

"Yes," said Sue. "I'm pretty sure it's a Spanish Doubloon from a pirate's treasure. See the cross? I imagine it was minted sometime around 1700 or so. They turn up once in a while on the beaches of the islands, but finding one on shore is unusual."

"How do you think it got here?" asked McKenna.

"I imagine that it's part of the treasure of a pirate named Sandy Gordon. He was Martha's husband. The British Navy hanged him. Gordon marooned Martha on White Island to guard his treasure."

"Why would she remain?" asked Mom.

"It's a long story," said Sue. "It's a legend. Come on. I'll tell you as we head back to Portsmouth." They reached the inflatable. Sue turned to McKenna. "One other thing," she said.

"What?" asked McKenna, still shaken by the encounter with the Ghost of White Island. "'You will return,'" said Sue.

Luke chimed in at this point, "So did she go back?"

Mara responded with a grin, "Why don't you just be patient and listen? There is still a lot more to this entire tale. And now we are going back to the year 1715. Pay close attention."

PART 11

CHAPTER THREE

The Atlantic Ocean, 1715
The *Regent*

Rabbi Sholem Levin sat on the deck of the tiny ship *Regent* that was carrying him from his former home in Ireland to the new world. He still felt traces of seasickness that had gripped him for the first few days of the voyage as the ship pitched up and down on the North Atlantic.

He was leaving his home in Ireland behind for good, but he felt no regret about it. The life of a Jew in England, in Scotland or in Ireland had been difficult.

Sholem sighed. His great-grandfather and his family and most of the Jews had been expelled from England because Dr. Roderigo Lopez, a Spanish Jew, had been convicted—maybe by mistake—of trying to assassinate Queen Elizabeth in 1594, years before. The persecutions and expulsions of the Jews began, as if an entire race had been responsible for one man's crime.

Sholem hoped things would be better in the American colonies. Boston was the ship's destination, but Sholem would be happy to settle anywhere in the New World. Plantations and businesses were thriving.

People told him that a man could find work in the largest cities. In addition to his work as a rabbi, he was a superb carpenter.

What mattered the most, though, were the family treasures that Sholem was carrying to the new world: two leather cases, one of which contained an ancient wooden staff and another that contained a translucent red rock. Their value was priceless.

According to legend, the rock—known to ancient Israel as the Urim and Thummin—was a channel to God. The staff was just as famous. Both were assumed lost to the nation of Israel...

Yet they were not lost even though at this time there was no nation. Israel had not existed as a state for more than 1,600 years. Jerusalem, the destroyed city that was the heart and soul of Israel, was lost to the Jews forever, to all evidence. Yet not forgotten. Every year the Passover feast concluded with the prayer, "Next year in Jerusalem."

Sholem, sitting alone, recited in Hebrew the words of Psalm 137: *"If I forget you, Jerusalem, may my right hand forget its skill. May my tongue stick to the roof of my mouth."*

The Fourth Night, Sholem believed, was coming.

The First Night was the night of creation. The Second Night was the giving of the covenant to Sholem's ancestor, Abraham, the father of many nations. The Third Night was the night of the Passover, when the great prophet Moses led the children of Israel out of Egypt. The Fourth Night would see the return of Israel to the land. The High Priest would again enter the temple, accompanied by the priest of the Lamb of God.

For Sholem and his fellow Jews held out the hope that someday the temple would again rise on Mount Moria. On that day, Praise songs would again echo through the rebuilt temple; the fragrant smell of the burnt offerings would rise as the priests again sacrificed to the God of Abraham, Isaac and Jacob.

Many of the great treasures were lost, perhaps destroyed when Israel suffered invasions of pagan armies. Gone were the golden altar of incense, the golden candlesticks, and the greatest treasure, the Ark of the Covenant.

But two of the treasures had survived. Sholem grinned, thinking about how he obtained them.

Sholem leaned against the rail on the quarterdeck and thought of the miserable first three days of his journey. Never had he been so sick. Though he was a carpenter by trade, he often worked as a shipwright. *How ironic. Jews should never go to sea*, he thought. Well, this was his last trip—

A loud crash knocked him off his feet. Something slammed into the side of the ship and wood splinters flew everywhere. *Regent* rocked with the impact. Now, screams of terror rose from the passengers.

Sholem Levin struggled to his feet. He spied a monstrous ship off the port bow. The Jolly Roger, a pirate flag, flew from the mast of the huge ship. Flashes of fire burst from the cannon ports. Then he heard the din of a thousand thunderclaps.

Again, cannonballs slammed into *Regent*. As it rocked and turned to flee, the little ship returned fire. Smoke and the smell of exploded gunpowder filled Sholem's nostrils. He could see, however, that the defense of *Regent* would be useless. *Regent* surrendered within minutes.

Sholem ran down to his bunk and retrieved his treasures. He slipped the leather case with the red stone into one pocket of his coat and his copy of the *Tanach*, the Hebrew Bible, into the other. He clutched the staff to his chest and hurried back to the main deck.

When he emerged into the sunlight, the pirates had begun to swarm aboard. They threatened the passengers and crew with swords and pistols. The victims lined up with their hands raised. As they stood terrified, the pirate captain came aboard.

He had flaming red hair and wore an ill-fitting red uniform.

Sholem watched the pirate smooth the uniform and his hair, the criminal's self-importance evident in every movement.

The murders began when the pirate crew lined up the passengers and crew of *Regent*. The captain and first officer died at once, thrown overboard to drown. Sholem felt his stomach knot at the nauseating brutality.

The pirate captain watched as his men stripped the ship and its passengers of anything of value. If a passenger or a crewman had nothing to give, two or three pirates would seize him and throw him overboard.

At last the pirate captain stood before Sholem. A pirate slammed a sword against Sholem's neck and forced him to empty his pockets. "What are these?" shouted the captain, pointing to Sholem's treasures.

"Please. They have no value except to my people. You cannot use them. Nor can I. Yet they must not be lost. Please," Sholem begged the redheaded criminal.

The pirate regarded him for a few moments. "You're a Jew."

"Yes."

The captain sneered with contempt and gestured to the pirate behind Sholem. The man kicked Sholem behind his knees and he fell to the deck. The villain drew back his sword, ready to strike off Sholem's head.

"Wait," cried Sholem. "Please promise to protect the treasures, at least."

The pirate captain grunted. "You have more fear for these objects than for yourself."

"Yes, that's true. They are far more important than I am."

The captain nodded to the crewman, who put away his sword. The man leaned forward and took Sholem's treasures, examining them. As the man turned to go, Sholem's eyes filled with tears. He began to chant under his breath the words that had been the password of his people for millennia. *"Shema Yisrael, Adonai elohenu, Adonai echad."*

"What are you saying?" demanded the pirate captain.

"It is called the *Shema*," Sholem said.

"What language?"

"Hebrew."

"What does it mean?"

Sholem gave the best translation he could. *"'Hear, O Israel, the Lord our God, the Lord is one.'"*

The captain grunted and waved his thumb at the crewman, who nodded and pulled the red stone from its leather case. He examined it, turning it this way and that. Then he held it to the sunlight.

A bolt of red light shot from the stone into the center of his chest. He turned toward the pirate leader. "Captain?" he muttered. His eyes rolled back into his head. He crashed face forward onto the deck, fingers still clutching the stone.

All movement on the ship stopped. The ship grew silent. All eyes stared at the dead man, then at their captain.

The redheaded man stood with his mouth open, eyes wide. He turned back to Sholem. "What did you do?"

"I did nothing. I cannot use the stone." Sholem walked to the corpse. He removed the stone from the dead fingers and returned it to its leather pouch.

"What is your trade?" barked the captain.

"I am a rabbi. That means teacher," Sholem explained, seeing the puzzled look on the Captain's face. "Also, I support myself as a carpenter and shipwright."

The captain nodded to two of his men. "Watkins. Sturdevant. Tie him and bring him."

The two men, looking apprehensive, lashed Sholem and led him to the side of the ship. They tied a rope around his waist. The two pirates lifted him and threw him into the ocean.

Sholem, hands tied, dropped like a shot below the surface. Just as he began to panic he jerked to a stop. The rope jolted the breath out of him. He choked and inhaled water. In that moment he assumed he was dead. He focused his mind on the Eternal. *Shema Yisrael, Adonai elohenu, Adonai echad–*

*****

Sholem began to regain consciousness, his head throbbing with pain. Though he was still tied up, he was lying flat on the deck of a ship. He choked again. He lifted his head and tried to sit up.

"No," said a commanding female voice. "No, you must not move."

Sholem looked up at the voice. To his intense surprise, he saw the deep blue eyes of a teenage girl with a kind, sympathetic face and striking copper-colored hair who knelt beside him. She had many bruises on her arms and face, including a black eye. She began untying his arms and legs.

Sholem, sensitive and kind, realized that the girl was frightened, but hid her fear well. He managed to smile.

"You will be all right," she assured him, taking charge of the situation. A few months on the pirate ship had given her some boldness needed to survive. "Do not try to speak yet."

Sholem took a deep breath. His lungs and ribs ached, and he coughed a few times. The girl laid a gentle hand on his forehead. "What ship is this?" he whispered.

"You are aboard *The Flying Scot*, under the command of Captain Gordon. The captain believes I am his wife."

"What do you mean?" Sholem asked her.

"I will explain another time. Be quiet if you wish to live."

Sholem took a long look at the girl who wore the female version of a pirate outfit: leather, high boots, weapons in her belt and Cross-bandoliers. He began to wonder if he could trust her. He turned his head to the right and saw the two leather cases and his copy of *Tanach* sitting next to him. "Where are we going?"

"We are headed to White Island off the coast of New Hampshire."

"America?"

"Yes. White Island serves as his hideout."

"Why did not your—ah—the pirates kill me?"

"Gordon needs carpenters to repair the ship. It took a beating in a recent battle. The men are afraid of these objects of yours," she said, pointing to the leather cases. "They hope to ransom you and the objects."

"But I have no friends in the New World."

"I see." Her brow wrinkled and she put a finger to her mouth. She regarded him for some time. "Who are you?"

"My name is Sholem Levin. I am a Jewish rabbi."

"How do you do?" she said, and shook his hand. "My name is Martha. I prefer to think of myself as Martha Herring."

"I understand," he said. He could see she had spirit and courage, as well as a keen mind. She would not surrender to a forced marriage without a fight. Nor would the marriage be a pleasant one for the pirate captain. The captain, little more than a bullying, preening popinjay, probably resorted to beating her to destroy her spirit.

She pointed to the leather cases. "I will try to persuade him to let me have your treasures. Would you tell me what these objects are?"

He hesitated, unsure of her loyalty to the pirate captain despite the bruises on her face and arms. He didn't want to give the criminals more information than he had to.

She appeared to misunderstand his indecision and looked around. "No one is here. You can talk now."

He couldn't imagine that this young woman had an ounce of dishonesty about her. He nodded. "Do you know anything about the Bible?"

"Only a little," she admitted. "I would love to learn, though."

He heard the note of eagerness in her voice. "Let me tell you about my ancestor, Moses."

Martha smiled and shifted her position. It was clear that she was thrilled to hear a story. He related how Moses and his brother Aaron had come to Pharaoh's palace to ask him to release the enslaved Hebrews. The king had refused. Aaron demonstrated the power of the staff.

Martha stared at Sholem, her eyes wide as he completed the story. "You mean Aaron turned this staff into a monster?"

He smiled at her innocence. "Not quite. The Eternal performed the miracle. But Aaron would become the High Priest of all Israel."

"Tell me another story," she said, her voice almost pleading. His heart broke as he sensed her appalling loneliness. He gave her hand a gentle squeeze as he began another story.

He related how Pharaoh had come to bathe in the waters of

the Nile. Moses had come to him again. When Pharaoh refused to release the Hebrews, Aaron had touched the staff to the surface of the river. The Nile turned to blood.

The young woman stared at him in silence as Sholem finished telling the story.

"So, this staff belonged to Moses?" she said, her voice hushed.

"Yes," he said, "and then to Aaron and all the High Priests until the time of Elijah. So did the Urim Stone," he nodded to the other leather case. "The high priests were able to use it to determine the will of The Eternal."

"Very well," she said. She sat up, looking inspired and confident. "Let me take the objects ashore with me at White Island. I can protect them there."

"Are you not afraid of the staff and the rock?"

"Yes. But I can touch them without harm coming to me."

Sholem's eyes widened. "I am surprised," he admitted. "Perhaps only the wicked cannot touch these items."

She shrugged. "Try to be calm," she said, patting his arm. "We have several days to go until we see White Island. We can talk later."

Sholem spoke with Martha as often as he could during the trip to the Isle of Shoals. He spent hours rebuilding and repairing the ship. As he worked, she would sit with him. He told her story after story about the history of his people. Her curious mind and desire to learn all she could impressed him. They became fast friends.

One night, *The Flying Scot* stood in sight of land. Sholem saw the cold bleak rock known as White Island looming in the moonlight.

Martha came to Sholem in the darkness. "I have to go in the morning," she said as the crew dropped anchor. "I will take the staff and stone with me."

"Very well," he said.

"Now that I am going to have Gordon's baby," she said, "perhaps these objects will help protect me."

"Perhaps," he agreed, startled at her announcement. He hadn't really known that she was pregnant. "Thank you."

"Sholem," she asked, "could I learn to use them?"

He shook his head. "I am all but certain you cannot. Ancient tradition says that only one person alive can use them, and I am not he. But please keep them safe. Please."

She smiled. "I will do my best," she agreed.

"No," he said and held out the *Tanach*. "This is vital. My family has watched over them for centuries. Please swear that you shall care for them."

She hesitated but then laid her hand on the outstretched book. She said, "Sholem. I promise I shall make sure they are safe until the rightful owner comes for them." She put the Tanach into her pocket.

"Martha?" yelled Gordon.

"I am here," she called back. "Just getting some air." In the morning the pirates rowed Martha ashore.

Sholem saw the fear on her face, her terror at being marooned on this miserable rock. As he waved goodbye, he felt hot tears in his eyes.

Martha, he was certain, would be true to her vow. He was also sure that he would miss the young woman. She was a ray of goodness and kindness penetrating the darkness of a ship of misery filled with murderers and criminals.

Sholem sighed and turned back to his chores of repairing the damage to *the Flying Scot.*

Macey was outraged at the details Mara shared with them. "How could anyone be so mean? And she was going to have a baby and be left all alone?"

"Yes," replied Mara. "Though he had the crew build a small cabin to shelter her, it was hardly adequate against the harsh Atlantic weather. Now, another man enters the story. His name is Owen McClelland. Let us see how he will affect all that has happened."

CHAPTER FOUR

On the fourth of March in 1715, Owen McClelland took his small boat out to fish off the coast of New Hampshire, taking advantage of the uncharacteristic warmth of the day, the calm sea, and the expanse of blue sky. The cold spray from the waves made him laugh.

Since the death of his father two years ago, Owen had been earning a living in town as a carpenter and shipwright. He took care of his mother and two younger brothers. He supplemented his family's food by fishing in the Atlantic off the chain of islands known as the Isle of Shoals. His mother made no secret at how proud she was of him.

Owen headed his little skiff toward White Island. As he sailed, he hauled in a few smaller fish, an ocean perch and a herring. They would make a sparse dinner that night.

Soon he came within sight of White Island. To his surprise, he saw smoke rising from a small cabin constructed from rock and with a metal roof. He didn't know that anybody lived out on White Island. Nor could he imagine why anyone would *want* a home on the barren rock.

As he stared at the cabin, his boat hit a submerged boulder. The boat pitched to the right, soaking him and all but capsizing the boat. He fought hard not to panic for a moment or two.

He seized a bucket and bailed as fast as he could. Then he turned to the rear of the boat, and realized that he'd snapped the handle of the rudder on his little sailboat. So he was not only was taking on water, but now had no way to steer the little boat.

Drenched with icy ocean water and freezing cold, he broke out the oars. He labored hard, feeling warmth spread as his muscles were exercised. In a few moments, he managed to row ashore in a small sheltered cove at White Island. He decided to go to the cabin and ask to borrow some tools to repair the handle of the rudder.

When he knocked, a pretty young woman opened the door a crack and peered out at him, fear evident in her eyes. Owen, trying hard not to shiver, dragged his hat from his head and introduced himself. "Please excuse me," he said, his teeth chattering. "I had an accident in my skiff. May I—"

She opened the door wide for him. "Sir," she interrupted. "Please, you are wet. Yes, of course you must come in." Entering the cabin, he noticed that she was several months pregnant.

Owen walked in and sat in a chair she drew up by the fire. He stripped off his soaking clothes and the girl hung them to dry before the fire. She gave him a blanket to wrap around his shoulders. "I have some tea brewing now. It will warm you."

"Thank you," he said.

"My name is Martha Herring," she said. "I am married to a man named Sandy Gordon. He is not here, though I do expect him."

"May I wait for him, Mistress Gordon?" asked Owen, trying to keep his teeth from chattering. "I need–"

Her face flushed. "Please do not call me Mistress Gordon," she interrupted in a fiery tone. "He forced me to marry him."

Owen blinked with surprise. "Forced?"

"Yes, and with a drawn pistol," she said, her eyes flashing with indignity. Then she drew a deep breath and cast her eyes down. "I apologize. You would not care to hear about my life–"

"On the contrary," said Owen. "I should be honored to hear."

Martha looked up at him and studied his face for a time. At last, she seemed to make up her mind to tell him. "I am British. My father was the captain of a privateer ship called *Porpoise*. Last year he took me to sea with him."

"Why?" asked Owen. *The open sea is no place for a young woman*, he thought. She stared at the fire again. He could see her debating with herself about what to tell him. It occurred to him that he sat in the presence of the most beautiful woman he'd ever seen. Yet he could feel the appalling loneliness in her soul. And— what? Fear?

She tucked a wisp of hair behind her ear. She sat composing a statement. "My mother died of the fever, sir," she said at last. "I had no relatives with whom I could stay. I was but fourteen then. My father intended to go to the Barbary Coast to fight the Algerian pirates."

"So, he brought you along." Owen couldn't believe the father had done such a foolish thing. She nodded.

"About three weeks into the voyage I met the carpenter's mate, Sandy Gordon."

Now Owen had warmed enough so that his mind cleared. He lifted a hand. "Do you mean you are married to Sandy Gordon the pirate?"

"Yes," said Martha, rising and crossing to the fire. She took a pad and removed a kettle from the fire and added some tea.

Owen, now frightened, wished he could leave at once. Gordon ranked as one of the most feared brigands operating off the American Atlantic Coast. But Owen knew he had to wait until he dried off somewhat. If he went out into the cool air still drenched, he could catch pneumonia.

He also struggled not to curse her husband for leaving this young woman alone in the late winter weather on this bleak rock. *What sort of a monster would do such a thing? She must be terrified all the time. Storms ravage this rock and ferocious winds lash this cabin.* He sensed that holding on to sanity would be a daily struggle for her.

Martha invited him to turn his chair to the small table. As she waited for the tea to steep, she told him where she was from, and a little about her father, John Herring.

"Sandy Gordon misunderstood my attempt to be friendly," said Martha. "He came to my cabin when my father was occupied with a matter of ship's discipline. He pushed his way in. It became obvious he thought I was attracted to him and he tried to kiss me.

"However, the first mate heard my screams and came to my aid. My father had Gordon dragged to a cannon. The bosun's mate lashed him seventy-two times."

"Seventy-two lashes!" said Owen, appalled. His fear began to subside in his compassion for his hostess. "And he survived?"

"Yes," she said. "He fell unconscious at the twentieth stroke. My father imprisoned him below decks for thirty days." She poured him a large mug of the heavy fragrant tea and took a smaller one for herself.

They drank together for a few moments. The liquid warmed him but he kept glancing toward the door, anxious that Gordon might return.

"When he was released from his prison, he'd become bitter

and angry," Martha said. "He gathered around him other discontented men. They mutinied and captured my father. Those who continued to be loyal to my father were thrown overboard." Owen shook his head in disbelief.

"Gordon's men dragged my father to the same cannon where my husband—" her face twisted with anger—"whipped my father to death." Her voice faltered and tears rose in her eyes as she relived the horror of the episode.

Owen took her hands in his. He murmured sympathy until Martha composed herself. "And you saw all this?" he asked.

"Yes," said Martha. "They forced me to watch." She dabbed a handkerchief at her eyes. "When my father was dead, Gordon nodded to three men who threw my father's body overboard."

Owen covered her hand with his and looked in her eyes. "And then he came to claim you as his own," said Owen, completing her story for her.

Martha looked downward and nodded her head in agreement. "Yes, and he forced me to wear the clothes of a pirate. When I came to this island, I brought my normal clothing with me."

They sipped the tea in silence for a few moments. "My husband wasted no time in turning *Porpoise* into a pirate ship," she continued. "He captured several ships.

"Despite his success, he was not well liked by his men since he felt that he was entitled to all the loot for himself. He paid the men on the ship a salary."

"Salaries on a pirate ship? I always thought that they split any treasure they stole," said Owen. His mind was reeling at the young woman's story.

She shrugged. "They resented him within a few months. He

became a tyrant. He had his closest allies throw anyone who questioned him overboard." Owen shuddered at the picture.

"At last the crew rebelled," continued Martha. "At first I feared they would kill us both. They were merciful, I think, because of me. By then my pregnancy had become obvious. The crew marooned us on the coast of Scotland, a mile or two from a small village." Martha rose and re-filled the cups.

"How did you survive?"

"Gordon had some money he'd hidden away. I tried to escape many times. He tied me to a bunk. On occasion, he would strike me."

"Your face is bruised, Martha," he said. "As well as your arms."

"Oh," she said, trying to dismiss the concern in his voice. "It is nothing."

"Did Gordon do that to you?"

"Please, Mr. McClelland, do not be concerned."

He grunted. *At least he didn't throw her overboard,* he thought. "How did you get here?" asked Owen.

"Captain Edward Teach found us in Scotland."

"Teach? Do you mean—"

"Yes," she replied with a shudder. "Blackbeard."

Owen felt his stomach tighten again. His hand trembled as he lifted the cup to his lips. Martha appeared lost in thought, silent for a few moments. At last she took a sip and began to talk again. "We were taken aboard *Queen Anne's Revenge,* Teach's ship. Not many days later *Revenge* joined battle with a British warship named *Renown.* Gordon's ferocity in the battle impressed Teach. When the battle concluded, the pirates threw the British officers overboard."

"A novel way to treat helpless captives," said Owen, feeling disgust. "It sounds like that is their answer for everything."

"Yes," she said, shrugging in agreement. "Gordon pressed the rest of the survivors into his crew, since he threatened to throw them overboard if they refused to join. Teach gave the ship over to my husband and he re-named it *The Flying Scot*. We parted company with *Revenge* and came to the island here."

"Why don't you leave?" asked Owen.

"They left me no boat. People sail by on occasion, but I have not been able to attract anyone's attention. Besides–" she bit her lip.

"Yes?" asked Owen.

"I swore an oath to guard this chest and these items." She pointed to a large sea chest on the wall opposite to the door. Next to it was a leather case, well-worn and old, about four and one-half feet long. A small leather box sat on top of the chest.

"What are they?"

"The chest contains gold and jewelry stolen from several ships."

"Treasure?"

"Oh, yes."

"What of the two leather cases?"

"I can show them to you." She crossed the small room to the case and extracted a four-and-one-half- foot-long wooden pole, polished and well worn. She handed it to Owen.

Owen examined the staff. "The wood is almond, if I am not mistaken. I do some carpentry. Almond tree stems grow very straight like this. Some letters are carved into it, but I don't know what they say. I don't even recognize them. It isn't English."

"Can you read?" asked Martha.

"Yes," said Owen. "My mother insisted that I learn. She taught me. I read the Scripture in our church services in the village." He blushed as she looked at him in some admiration. "I—er—seem to have some gift for language. I have studied Greek and Latin as well."

"I wish I could read," she said. "I have nothing to occupy my time. A friend gave me this Bible."

She reached to the table next to her chair and handed him a small leather-bound book. He accepted it and began to leaf through it. He couldn't read the writing inside.

"I sleep with it," she went on. He glanced up and she returned his little grin. "It gives me much comfort. The nightmares are not so terrifying."

"This book does not seem to be a Bible," frowned Owen. "At least, it is not written in English. It appears to be valuable."

She knelt next to his chair and fumbled with the small jewelry box. Her closeness felt wonderful. In that moment, he realized that he wanted this woman next to him for the rest of his life.

He lifted a hand, wanting to stroke her lovely hair. He'd seen the bruises on her face and knew how she'd gotten them. He wanted to say, *No one would ever hurt you again, Martha. I promise it.*

He shrugged the impulse away. She was another man's wife, even if she had been forced into the marriage. He could not allow himself to think of anything beyond that.

Unaware of the effect she was having on him, she opened the small jewelry case. She handed Owen a small stone inscribed with letters similar to the ones he saw on the staff and in the book. Again, he couldn't read the letters.

The translucent stone seemed to be red crystal carved into an oval shape, bound with a band of gold. Owen held it up to the sunlight that streamed through the window.

"You can use the stone," Martha gasped.

Owen saw her staring at him. He looked down. His entire body was radiant with a pure red light.

He extended his hand to her and she took it. The glow expanded to surround both young people. He felt soothing warmth as he held her hand. He studied her eyes, blue and deep. She gave him a smile of peace, as if she were experiencing the feeling for the first time.

"You and I belong together," he said to her. He felt sure in his soul that he was speaking the truth in the purest form that it could be expressed by a human being.

"I feel it too," she agreed. "It is so clear. You and I are supposed to spend our lives with each other."

He couldn't take his eyes from hers in the beautiful glow. Right then he made a decision. "Come with me. We must leave this place. I promise that I will hide you so that you are safe. You cannot live with a pirate."

"I know," she said. Her voice trembled. He felt that she was afraid, but ready to take whatever steps were necessary. She put up her arms and he enfolded her. They kissed each other with loving devotion.

For the next several years, the memory of that kiss would be one of the few things that would sustain Owen's heart.

At last they drew back and Owen lowered the stone and put it into his pocket. As the perfect light faded, he found that his clothes were dry and warm. He felt filled with courage, unafraid and confident. She smiled up into his eyes.

He swallowed, trying to calm down. "I must fix my boat before we can go," he managed. "Do you have any tools, Martha?"

"Yes," she said. She hurried to the other side of the room and opened a small chest. She showed him hammers, augers, bits, nails and other tools. He selected a few.

"Pack some clothes," he told her. "We will hide in Portsmouth or go farther inland, or to Boston or New York. I can fix the rudder in no time."

Martha nodded. Her posture and attitude now reflected hope and newfound joy. She stepped forward and embraced him for a few seconds, giddy with excitement at an opportunity to get away from Gordon and this dreadful island.

Owen felt a trace of dizziness at the girl's touch. Now he said, "No one will ever hurt you again, Martha. I pledge it." She lifted a gentle hand to stroke his face.

He slid the book and the stone into the pocket of his coat and ran to the boat. Within ten minutes he had repaired the rudder.

He ran back to the cabin and threw open the door. "Martha," he called. Owen gasped. He saw five men standing there in seaman's clothing. The red-headed leader wore an ill-fitting red uniform.

The leader came forward with his pistol drawn. "Who are you?" asked the man, speaking with a severe Scottish brogue.

"My name is Owen McClelland," he said. "My boat hit a boulder and I was forced to came ashore to repair the rudder on my boat. Martha was kind enough to loan me these tools." He held them up.

"You were here alone with my wife?" thundered the man,

his voice booming with anger.

Now, Owen understood the seriousness of his situation. The man confronting him was Sandy Gordon, a vicious killer and pirate. "For a few moments, yes. My boat almost capsized. I was soaked with seawater. Martha allowed me to dry my clothes and gave me hot tea."

"Did you take advantage of her?" asked the man, his face red and his eyes flaming with rage.

"Of course not," said Owen, his own anger now rising.

"No!" screamed Martha as the pirate placed the muzzle of the gun against Owen's forehead. "He has been a perfect gentleman."

Owen knew that Gordon would not hesitate to shoot him. He looked at Martha. Three men held the weeping young woman back.

Owen reached into his pocket and touched the mysterious stone. Nervousness and fear vanished. He smiled at Martha and nodded. She calmed a bit. He drew himself up to his full height, unafraid, and stared into the pirate's eyes.

Gordon lowered his eyes and his pistol. "What do you do besides searching out deserted islands?"

He spoke without thinking. "I work as a shipwright in Portsmouth."

Gordon nodded and a smirk came over his face. "Dunbar, take him to the ship. I shall be there in a moment. I must see to my wife."

"Aye, sir," said the one named Dunbar. Two of the men released Martha. They bound and gagged Owen and dragged him down a path to a ship's boat.

Owen understood. Gordon planned to press him into his

pirate crew. The men rowed him out to a huge vessel. People on the ship threw down a rope, which the men in the boat tied around his waist. They hoisted Owen aboard.

Several men dragged him to a grate that was fastened to a mast. The pirates spread-eagled him and tied his hands and feet to the grate so that he was incapable of movement, and left in that condition for quite some time. He was in distress, his arms leaden and aching, and his heart throbbing with horror over what that hideous man was doing to Martha. Would she be beaten or punished in some way for letting him into the cabin?

CHAPTER FIVE

"What are you going to do with him?" asked Martha, trying to keep her voice neutral. "Mr. McClelland. He treated me with great kindness. He offered to take me to the mainland."

"What for?"

"I did not know when you were returning. My supplies are low. I intended to purchase some food and bring back some water," she lied. She'd had no intention of returning to the loathsome cabin on the dismal rock. But now, Owen's life was in jeopardy. Gordon wouldn't hesitate to throw Owen overboard if he suspected that they had planned to go ashore and hide from him.

"I will send more provisions and water over. I will be back in a few weeks. Meantime do not forget your promise."

He opened the door and strode away without closing the door behind him. He made his way down to the skiff that was waiting for him.

Martha stood and realized that she had changed. Not physically, but in every other way. She felt confident, more determined. Now, she knew her mind had expanded. She had become wiser, more mature—

And no longer was she afraid.

It was the stone. The red light had enveloped her and in those moments, all fear, all anger, all resentment had vanished. She was no longer a scared girl. She had become a fearless, determined woman.

In a few moments the boat's skiff returned, bringing supplies for her. She didn't return to the cabin but hid behind a boulder so that the pirates wouldn't see her. These men were terrified of Gordon but still, she did not trust them.

When they returned to the ship, she emerged from behind the rock. She walked down a little path to the southeast side of the island and watched as *The Flying Scot* hoisted anchor and unfurled sail.

She wept, knowing what Gordon would do to Owen. The horror overwhelmed her and she fell to her knees. *Adonai*, she prayed as Sholem had taught her, *the God of Abraham, Isaac and Jacob, please protect him. Don't let him be destroyed.*

Aloud, she said, "He will return."

✳✳✳✳✳

Owen heard voices and turned his head. He saw Gordon approaching. "McClelland, is it?" said the pirate.

"Yes."

"When you speak to me, you will say, 'Aye Sir,'" said the man. "I am Captain Gordon." Gordon was dressed in the uniform of a captain of the Royal Guard. The red of his uniform exaggerated his red hair and ruddy complexion. The pirate removed his coat.

Owen noticed the jacket of his uniform was stretched so tight across his belly that the buttons were about to pop off. The pirate looked so ridiculous in his outfit, Owen fought to suppress a laugh, even in these dire circumstances.

"You will address me as 'Sir', *do you understand!*"

"Yes—I mean aye, sir." The Captain gestured to two of the men standing next to the grate. One produced a knife and cut a small hole in the back of Owen's shirt. Then he ripped the fabric from waist to neck and laid the skin bare.

Luke interrupted Mara. "What is he going to do to Owen? I mean doesn't he want him to help repair the ship?"

Mara replied, "I am afraid Gordon gave the order to have Owen whipped."

"But he didn't do anything," protested Macey.

"I am sure that made little difference to Gordon. He was mean and cruel and was making a statement about who was in control of Owen's life and the lives of all the other crew as well," explained Mara. "Now let's go back and see what is going on with Martha at this point."

CHAPTER SIX

Martha wept as she remembered her screams when her father died under Gordon's lash. "Good-bye, Owen," she sobbed, standing at the top of White Island, watching *The Flying Scot* sailing away. "Why could you not have come to my prison yesterday?" she wondered aloud, remorse filling her soul.

The skiff tied in the cove on the western side of the island had to be Owen's. The pirates had come in from the east and hadn't seen it.

If only I knew how to sail, she thought, *I could be free and safe in a few hours. I could take enough money to hide–*

Martha pushed the notion aside. At that moment, she felt a sharp pain in her abdomen.

Oh no, she thought. *The baby cannot come now. I do not know what to do.*

Terror seized her. She knew well that many babies died in childbirth. *She* could die. She forced the terror down and thought about Owen, and the lovely red light of the Urim Stone. A gentle, calm peace enveloped her.

Somehow, she knew she would never have to be afraid again.

To her relief, the pain eased and didn't recur. She calmed down and her panic was replaced by a newfound confidence. She *had* to get off the island.

She made herself a quick promise to escape from her miserable prison. She spent the rest of the day gathering driftwood and hauling it to the top of the island.

Back at the cabin she fixed a meager dinner and went to bed early. She searched for Sholem's book, but then remembered that Owen had taken it with him.

She knew what she needed to do. In the morning, she dug a pit in the sand at low tide.

Her husband had brought a load of treasure with him and dumped it into the chest. She loaded as much of the loot as she could carry into a bag made of sailcloth, and then dragged it down the path to the beach. Her arms and legs ached, despite trying to do the work with as little effort as possible.

A single doubloon fell from a tiny hole in the sack. It hit a small patch of sand, bounced and rolled behind a rock. She never noticed the loss of the small coin that would be discovered for three hundred years later by another girl visiting the island.

At last she lowered the chest with the rest of the treasure into the pit. She covered the chest with sand and memorized the location of the loot.

Then she went to the southern tip of the island and built a fire. She sat next to the fire and waited. If a boat came by, she would be ready.

"Oh, the girl that found the coin was McKenna, wasn't it? The girl you just told us about," announced Macey.

"Well, I am glad you are paying attention to my story," Mara laughed. She continued the adventure, now returning to the plight of Owen.

*****

Consciousness returned to Owen in the dark. As his eyes adjusted, he saw that he was in the hold of a ship. He tried to stand but found that he was chained to the wall.

He felt the motion of the sea. The ship must be under sail, leaving the island, he thought.

Owen's first concern was for his mother. Tears rose to his eyes as he imagined how upset she would be. Searching parties would go out. They would find his boat at White Island and would assume he had fallen overboard and drowned.

He groaned to think of the agony of his family at his death. They would never guess that he'd been pressed into the service of a pirate.

He was young and strong even if he was in crippling pain, and decided he would desert at his first opportunity. Having grown up by the ocean, he could swim well, unlike most of the sailors of his time.

But it would be several days before he could move with the pain in his back, shoulders, and rump from his whipping.

"You are awake, lad," said a voice in the darkness.

"Aye," he said. His throat ached with the hoarseness brought on by his screams.

"Drink this," said the voice. Owen felt a rough pewter cup pushed into his hands.

"What is it?"

"A mixture of rum and opium. It will dull the pain," said the voice. "Drink it at once in one gulp."

Owen drank the foul mixture and handed the cup back. In moments the pain came closer to being bearable.

"Who are you?" he asked the voice. "Levin," said the voice. "Sholem Levin." "My name is Owen McClelland, from Portsmouth."

The two men shook hands. "Where are we?" Owen asked.

"In the hold of *The Flying Scot*, Captain Gordon. He ordered me to describe your duties on the ship." Owen felt in his pocket and found the strange stone from the cabin on White Island. He showed it to Sholem. "How did you get this?" asked Sholem, wide-eyed and astonished at seeing the stone. Owen told him the story. Sholem nodded. "I gave it to Martha for safekeeping. I am glad she gave it to you. I can see that you are no thief."

As Owen's eyes adjusted to the darkness, he saw a faint glow of sunlight through a crack in the deck above.

He held the stone to the light. The small cabin lit up with a warm red light.

"You can use the stone," exclaimed Sholem Levin, surprise and excitement evident in his voice.

"Yes," said Owen. He studied the man standing before him. The man named Sholem was perhaps a few years older than Owen. His eyes reflected gentle kindness. "You are no pirate," Owen remarked.

"I am a teacher," said Levin. "Gordon hijacked me from a ship a few weeks ago. I support myself as a shipwright. Gordon told me that is your trade as well."

"Yes," said Owen.

"Gordon is a good sailor, but he needs people to repair his vessel after a battle. I have been doing so. You and I will work together."

"Aye. Where are we going?" Owen asked.

"I do not know," said Levin. Then he looked into the light and checked himself. "No. I do know. We are going into battle."

"This ship will be defeated," said Owen. "Gordon will die."

"You and I will survive though," said Levin.

"Yes. All others will die in battle or be hanged."

"Should we warn the captain?"

"No. This is inevitable." Owen and Levin nodded to each other. Owen put the stone away. The red light faded but he could still see Sholem's face, glowing with the soft red light. They sat and continued to talk.

"Sholem, are you Jewish?"

The other man laughed. "Oh yes."

Owen pulled the leather-bound book from his coat pocket. He handed it to Levin and admitted that he didn't know what the book was. "Martha gave it to me to hold until we could escape the island. Her husband returned before we could get away."

Sholem gave him a little nod. "That is quite unfortunate. I gave it to Martha for safekeeping. You are welcome to it. It is a copy of the *Tanach*."

"The what?"

"You might call it the Jewish Bible."

"You mean the Old Testament?" asked Owen.

Levin chuckled. "I guess so. It's written in Hebrew."

"No wonder I could not read it."

Sholem asked, "Would you like to learn?"

They agreed that Owen would begin his study of Hebrew at once. As they talked, Owen realized that his back didn't hurt. Sholem looked puzzled, but asked to examine him.

"Whatever he did to you, Owen," said Sholem, "you seem to be fine now. I see no trace of bleeding or welts."

The two men stared at each other, bewildered. "How can that be?" asked Owen.

"The stone," smiled Sholem. "I didn't realize it had such power, I guess."

CHAPTER SEVEN

Two days later, *The Flying Scot* attacked a small passenger ship named *The Lark*. In the midst of the battle a British ship, HMS *Repulse*, joined the fray. The two warships battled. Gordon proved no match for the Royal Marines who boarded the ship and took the surviving pirates onto *Repulse* for trial.

Owen stood next to Sholem, their hands tied behind them. Owen's knees were weak with fear. He knew too well that the British Navy hanged pirates without mercy. Although he reminded himself that the stone had predicted that he and Sholem would survive, he couldn't stop trembling.

Justice was swift. There was little mercy for pirates on the high sea and the British navy proceeded with their punishment. The hangings began almost at once.

Owen turned his eyes away from the grim scene. Instead he watched as the small passenger ship, the *Lark,* depart as it headed to America to dock in Boston. Regret filled his heart. Boston wasn't far from his home in Portsmouth. Ten miles of ocean separated the Portsmouth harbor from White Island and the girl named Martha. He felt a tear trickle down his cheek.

The British captain of *Repulse* stopped before Owen and Sholem and inspected the two young men. He appeared surprised to see a tear on the cheek of one of them. "Ringgold," he said to his first mate, "bring these two men to my cabin."

In the cabin, he spoke first to Sholem. "Who are you?" Levin told him his story. The captain looked suspicious. "You have only been aboard a few weeks, Rabbi Levin?"

"Aye, sir," said Levin. "Gordon kidnapped me from a passenger ship and compelled me to repair his vessel."

"What about you, lad?" asked the captain, turning to Owen.

Owen had to swallow before he could speak. "Gordon captured me two days ago, off White Island in the Isle of Shoals." Owen sketched out his story.

The captain looked back and forth between the two men. He crossed his arms and leaned back in his chair. "Can you prove this?"

Owen considered. "May I reach into my pocket?" he asked.

"Yes," nodded the Captain.

Owen removed the stone. He held it to the cabin's candlelight. In the next moment he and Levin were surrounded with a glowing red light. The captain's jaw dropped and his eyes widened. He sat up in his chair.

Owen spoke as the light produced a soft glow in the room. "Please, sir," he said. "Please send this stone to my mother in Portsmouth. It is precious beyond expression. I will write a letter to her to explain it–"

"You are not pirates," the captain decided. "Very well. You both will join our crew."

Owen lowered the stone, his mind whirling. He struggled to maintain his composure as he realized that the captain did not intend to hang him and his friend Sholem. His knees grew weak and he almost collapsed.

A sailor, seeing his weakness, grabbed his arm and held him upright. "Courage," said the man, his voice kind. The Captain gestured and the man untied Owen, then Sholem.

Owen thought of his mother, and then of sweet Martha still marooned on an island. "Please, sir."

"Yes?" said the captain.

"Sir, please let me go home to Portsmouth. My mother is widowed and I am the sole support of her and my brothers. I fear they will take ill and die without me."

The captain looked at the young man, still glowing with the red fire of the stone.

"No, McClelland, I cannot," said the captain, not without kindness. "We are now bound for the Barbary coast where we hope to capture more pirates and put an end to their tyranny. We can try to send a message if we encounter another ship. However, we cannot go back and *Lark* is miles from here now. I am sorry, Lad."

The boson's mate led Owen and Sholem to the crew quarters and assigned them each a hammock. Owen fought back tears, thinking of his mother and his brothers.

And Martha. He tried to fill his mind with thoughts of her, in hope that one day they would reunite.

The Flying Scot, the vessel that had been captured by Gordon, had been damaged beyond repair. The crew from *Repulse* stripped the black flag from its mainmast. The once-valiant ship sank beneath the waves, to a watery grave.

The captain of *The Flying Scot* died last of all. The marines dragged Sandy Gordon, blubbering and pleading, to the foredeck. The crew cut away and burned his stolen red uniform. He stood naked, begging for his life as his feet were placed in the chalked circle. A crewman put the black hood over Gordon's head and then the fatal rope. The hangman jerked the knot tight around his neck.

"My wife," Gordon choked, shouting over the drum roll. "She will die—" The rope cut off his words.

At sunset the sailors cut down his body and threw it overboard. Nor did Gordon receive a funeral.

As the weeks passed, Owen and Levin blended in with the crew. When he would be overcome with emotion, Owen would take his secret glass and hold it to a light source where he would find great comfort bathed in its warm radiance, and the pain in his heart would subside.

Having grown up by the ocean, Owen knew something about sailing. When he could set aside the worry about his mother and brothers, he came to love the sea and the ship he was on. The men aboard *Repulse* respected him as a hard worker, a decent man, and a good friend.

When they were off watch, Levin taught him to read Hebrew. Sholem was a tireless teacher and Owen's mind was fertile and active. He proved to have a fine gift for the language. To occupy his mind, he began to memorize the Book of Psalms, in Hebrew. Then he would translate the texts into English and memorize them. Each day, he found that he could do more. His heart calmed and he always slept better when he worked with the scriptures.

Luke interrupted, "Did they always kill pirates like that, I mean so quickly and by hanging?"

Mara looked directly at him and responded, "Yes, remember, pirates were without mercy to those they captured and had the blood of many an honest seaman on their hands. Do not feel sorry for them. They made a decision to follow evil and prey on innocent people to enrich themselves. When the British navy defeated a pirate ship, the justice was swift, and hanging was the punishment more often than not. Now, let us return to Martha. I think you will be pleased to learn what happens to her."

*****

Two days after the departure of *The Flying Scot*, Martha saw a fishing boat with two men aboard about a hundred yards from the island. She shouted to the two men and waved a pillowslip. They waved and steered to the shore.

"Who are you?" asked the first man when they came ashore.

"I am Martha McClelland," she lied. She worried about using either the name Herring or Gordon. She didn't know if the men would have heard about the fate of her father's ship, The *Porpoise*.

"McClelland?" said the second man, surprised. "Do you have relatives in Portsmouth?"

"Yes, my husband's family. His aunt invited my husband and me to come and live with her," she recited her rehearsed speech. "We were coming to meet her and her family but a pirate ship commanded by Captain Gordon captured us. They killed my husband. The pirates marooned me here when they found that I was—" She stroked her bulging belly.

"Gordon, eh?" said one of the men. "I am surprised he did not just throw you overboard." Martha shuddered. The man grew flustered and offered to apologize for scaring her. Martha waved the apology aside.

"Please," she said. "Take me to Portsmouth to my aunt. I will pay you."

The men agreed without hesitation. "I need to get some things, if you can wait a moment," she said. Martha hurried to the cabin. She grabbed a small bag filled with gold coins that she had stashed behind the fireplace, then picked up the staff and tucked it under her arm. She called to the men and they carried her small trunk to their little boat.

The men opened their sail and tacked back to the mainland. The waves weren't high, but she was no longer used to the motion and felt nauseous during most of the journey.

At Portsmouth, the men took her to the main pier. She struggled up the ladder. They introduced her to a man who would store her belongings in his warehouse by the dock. Then she received directions to Widow McClelland's home. She gave each of them a gold coin for their trouble, to their delight and gratitude.

The door opened after the first knock. A tall boy, perhaps ten years old and almost the image of Owen, stood there. His eyes widened with surprise. He managed a curious but polite smile. "Yes ma'am?"

"I am a friend of Owen's," said Martha.

The boy's eyebrows shut upward. "Do you know where he is? We are frantic. He has not been home—"

"Who is it, Charles?" said a woman's voice. Owen's mother, Grace McClelland, came forward. Her eyes were red with weeping and she clutched a handkerchief to her eyes.

"May I come in?" asked Martha.

A half hour later the sheriff sat in the small cottage listening as Martha related the story of Owen's kidnapping. "Gordon pressed Owen, eh?"

"Yes," Martha said.

"Well, Mrs. McClelland, this news gives us some hope. We assumed," he said, turning to Martha, "that Owen had drowned."

"No," Martha said. "I believe he is alive. He will try to escape, I know it."

When the sheriff had finished questioning her, he left. Mrs.

McClelland thanked Martha for coming to the house. "But Owen was our source of income. I do not know how we will continue until he returns."

Martha stood. "May we talk in private?"

"Yes, of course," said Mrs. McClelland. Martha took her outside and linked arms with the older woman.

Martha walked with her to the pier, a few streets away. Then she filled in what she had not told the sheriff. She told the story of her voyage on *Porpoise*. Gordon's mutiny. Her forced marriage to the pirate. Sholem. Gordon marooning her on White Island. How Owen had found her. Their plans to escape together.

"Gordon entrusted me to protect his treasure," she said. She reached into her bag and extracted a gold coin. "If you will hide me and let me stay with you until the baby comes, I will pay you and help with the household."

"My dear," said Mrs. McClelland, her voice tender, "I would let you stay with us for no charge at all. You are a friend of my son. I will never turn away anyone while I a m able to help."

Martha began to cry and her new friend embraced the frightened young woman. Martha began to understand why she had seen such great kindness in Owen and why she had confided in him with so little hesitation.

*****

In the first week of May news reached the New Hampshire colony that the Royal Navy had defeated Gordon's ship and the ship he had attacked, the *Lark*, had gone on to Boston.

Martha and Mrs. McClelland took a carriage to Boston, hoping to find some information about Owen. They found a man who had survived the battle. "Please," said Martha. "Do you have any news of a young man named McClelland?" She sketched Owen's story. "Or Levin?" she added.

"No," said the man. "The Captain of the British Warship assured us that he would hang all the pirates who were not killed in battle."

The pain was almost too much to bear as the two women returned to Portsmouth. Martha leaned on her new friend, weeping with grief while trying to console Mrs. McClelland. The British Navy had hanged Owen as a bloody pirate. *The love of my life*, she thought.

Also, her dear friend Sholem had died at the end of a humiliating rope, his wisdom, kindness and knowledge lost forever.

The night they returned to Portsmouth, Martha's labor began and she gave birth to a beautiful baby boy. Martha, overjoyed at the safe birth and her son's health, thought him handsome beyond hope. She couldn't stop staring at the baby's copper red hair and startling green eyes.

A curious word stuck in her mind. *Faerae*.

"What is his name, dear daughter?" asked Grace McClelland, wiping Martha's forehead with a damp cloth.

Martha said, "I am naming him in honor of my father, but also, a man with whom I talked for less than an hour. My son's name is John Owen McClelland."

CHAPTER EIGHT

Several months later *Repulse* engaged in a fierce battle off the coast of Algeria. No less than twelve small pirate vessels set upon the British warship.

The first volley of cannon fire killed the captain. The next assault took down the mast of the ship.

Algerian pirates boarded. Owen and Sholem fought side by side. At one point, two pirates overpowered Sholem. One forced Sholem into a kneeling position and the other lifted a rusty curved sword to strike off Levin's head. Owen swung his sword twice and the two pirates fell with mortal wounds.

Before the battle ended, the pirates had killed most of the men. They captured Owen and Sholem and a few others. They loaded them aboard a filthy ship and brought them ashore.

Owen and Sholem were sold into slavery. Each departed with his new master.

Owen languished in slavery as months, then years passed. The head slave, a cruel thug named Ashan, beat him, starved him, and forced him to work sixteen to eighteen-hour days. Still Owen labored every day to memorize and translate great portions of the *Tanach*. With his extraordinary gift of language, he managed to learn Arabic by listening to the other slaves.

One night, he realized it was the fifth anniversary of his captivity and sale into bondage. He took out his jewel, which along the *Tanach* were his only possessions and his only joy. The firelight created a red glow that surrounded him in ruby light. He had noticed some time ago that when he did this, he didn't feel quite as hungry or as thirsty. Ashan, the head slave, came out of the tent at that moment and caught the young American holding his jewel. "Give it to me," said the dull-witted brute.

Owen looked up, terrified of Ashan. He closed his hand over the stone.

All fear vanished. He scooped a handful of sand and stood up, confident and unafraid.

"No, I will not," said Owen in halting Arabic.

Ashan's face took on a sadistic grin of anticipation. He lashed at Owen with his whip. Owen dodged, grabbed the lash, and yanked Ashan off balance. Owen then threw the handful of sand into the thug's face.

Ashan choked and stumbled, pawing at his eyes. Owen charged. He buried his shoulder in the thug's gut and drove him back onto the sand. Ashan landed hard, the breath driven from his lungs. He reached to his side and drew out a long, double-edged knife. Ashan struggled to his feet and Owen broke his wrist with a powerful kick. The man grunted as the knife flew out of his hand.

He rose to his feet, holding his wrist and still unsteady on his feet. He stepped forward, ready to fight, still trying to clear his eyes. Ashan, bigger and stronger than Owen, reached to snatch the jewel away.

Owen knew the thug wouldn't hesitate to kill him with his bare hands. A torch on a long pole stood outside the entrance and Owen seized it. He placed his stone between the torch and Ashan.

A narrow beam of red light shot from the stone and hit Ashan in the forehead. He stood transfixed. A look of intense shock twisted his face and he screeched with terror. He clutched at his head as if trying to hold something inside. Then he crashed, face forward, to the ground.

Owen put the stone in his pocket. As he did so, two more slaves came out of the tent. They shrieked, "What happened?"

"I do not know," said Owen, replacing the torch. He wasn't lying. He hadn't the faintest idea what he had just done. "He threatened me and lashed at me with the whip. Then he got a strange expression on his face and fell over."

The other slaves summoned the master, who came out of the tent. He examined the dead body of Ashan.

The slaves rolled the body over. Fear contorted Ashan's face. His hands clutched his forehead as if someone were trying to tear his brain out. Still the body bore no other marks than the glowing red blotch in the center of his forehead.

Owen stood aside, feeling no guilt or shame, but baffled by the stone's response to Ashan's attack. He began to comprehend that somehow the stone had protected him from the brute.

The master ordered the other slaves to search Owen but they found no weapon, only a piece of red glass. The master held it up, turned it this way and that, and threw it back to Owen. Owen and two other men dragged the body into the desert, dug a shallow grave, and dumped in Ashan's body.

Owen followed the other two slaves back to the camp.

Back at the tent the master called to Owen and demanded water to wash his hands. He washed. Then again and again. "My hands are burning," he said to Owen. "What did you do?"

Owen replied in Arabic, "I did nothing. But I think I can ease the pain." The master nodded. Owen pulled the stone from his pouch and held it to the firelight.

In a few seconds the stone glowed in his hand. The aura

spread to the master and the old sheik's hands shone with red light as well. Owen closed his hand on the stone and the glow faded. The master looked at his hands, and then showed them to Owen. They were smooth, ungnarled, and pain free.

Owen stared at the sheik, then the stone. *How did I know to do that?*

The sheik, just as amazed, turned to the young American. He knew magic when he saw it and smiled at Owen for the first time. "Thank you, young man."

Owen gathered his wits and bowed. "I am glad I could serve you, sir."

"What is your name?" the sheik asked.

The next day, Owen's life began to change for the better. He took over running the desert sheik's household and began managing the man's business affairs. As Owen conducted the business of trading, the old sheik enjoyed unprecedented success.

To his delight, Owen learned that the sheik was not only able to read and write but was a prominent historian and scholar. When the sheik learned that Owen had a rich fertile mind, he taught the young man the Arabic written language, some of the history of the region, the Islamic faith, and the life of the desert. He made it clear that he enjoyed engaging Owen in conversation.

One night, after a profitable day of trading, the master called Owen to his side. "Owen," he asked the young man, "how can you tell who is lying and who is not?"

Owen grinned. "What do you mean?"

"You seem to know what these other men are thinking when bargaining —how low they will go, what they will accept—"

"It is a gift," said Owen, his hand stealing to the jewel in his pocket.

Mara paused to take a sip of her drink.

"Well, you aren't going to stop there, are you?" exclaimed Macey. "What happened to Sholem?"

"So I guess you want me to continue?" Mara smiled.

Both Luke and Macey bobbed their heads up and down in agreement.

"Perhaps we should see how Sholem is making out in his circumstances," suggested Mara.

CHAPTER NINE

Sholem Levin, now in slavery for several years, found himself in a caravan with a tribe of nomads who camped next to the Nile River. People from all over the region believed that the waters of the great river had life-giving and healing qualities. The slave master went to bathe in the river. He ordered Sholem to come along to guard him.

Sholem stood on the bank as the slave master entered the water. Out of the corner of his eye, Sholem saw movement. A crocodile entered the water not far from the slave master.

Without thinking, Sholem yelled a warning at the slave master and ran into the water, carrying a thick branch. The slave master turned, saw the crocodile and screamed with terror. He bolted for shore and had almost reached the bank as the crocodile lunged to attack.

Sholem leapt between the master and the crocodile. He struck the creature with the branch. The creature writhed and snarled and started for Sholem. Sholem lashed out at the creature again. The crocodile, roaring, turned aside. Again, Sholem struck and the creature swam away.

Sholem hurried out of the water and approached the slave master, who stood panting, pale with fear. "Are you all right, Sir?" Sholem asked.

The master stared at him. "Why did you save me?" he asked. "I have not been kind to you."

"All life is precious, Master," Sholem shrugged. "You trusted me to protect you."

The master continued to stare at him. "Can you swim?" he asked when he had regained his breath.

"Yes, sir," Sholem answered, puzzled by the question.

"Then swim to the other bank," he said. "Hide until it is dark. A path lies on the other side. Follow it to the village two days that way. Go to the house of my cousin Elim. Mention my name and show him this amulet"—he removed a gold chain from around his neck— "he will help you get away."

Sholem protested. "No, sir," he said. "You would be in deep trouble for allowing me to escape."

"You are concerned about me?" the slave master asked.

"I do not wish for you to be punished," Sholem returned.

"You are a noble man," he said. "It will be all right. I will say you gave your life to save me from the crocodile."

Sholem embraced him and ran into the river. He swam to the other bank, terrified that he would be attacked, but made it in safety. Some bulrushes grew along the river and he hid in them. He emerged from hiding at night and followed the slave master's direction, taking the path all the way to the village, arriving late the next day.

After making a few inquiries, Sholem located Elim, the slave master's cousin, who took Sholem with him in a boat. They followed the Nile to the Mediterranean. Sholem found a Dutch trading ship anchored in the bay and persuaded the captain to take him along.

Sholem sailed with the Dutch ship to Portugal, where he worked at his trade for some months. Then he took passage on a ship coming to America.

"I have to say," admitted Luke, "I don't know that I would have jumped in that water to save the slave master. Sholem is a much better

person than me."

Mara put a hand on his shoulder. "We never know our reaction in specific circumstances until tested, and one is never tested beyond their capability."

"What has happened with Martha during this time?" questioned Macey.

"Well, let me tell you about that," replied Mara.

*****

In Portsmouth, a unique gift became evident in Martha's son, John, one far superior than most normal people possess. One morning when he was five years old, he came to his mother's side in the small house and found her weeping. "What is it, Mama?"

Martha saw the concern on her son's face. She managed to smile at him. "I had a strange dream, John," she said. "I cannot remember all of it, but I dreamt of someone I have not seen in years."

The boy knelt on the settee next to his mother and took her face in his little hands. He stared deeply into her eyes and said, "Do not be scared."

Martha felt pleasant warmth in her mind. New colors and sounds and smells swirled and cleared. Then, to her complete amazement she saw the dream again.

She found herself sitting outside a tent under some strange looking trees, gazing into the depths of the mysterious red stone of long ago. Torchlight illuminated the area. A huge man emerged from a tent and stood over her. Martha understood that the man was a brutal thug and she was afraid. He spoke in a strange language, but Martha somehow understood what he said. "Give it to me."

"No," she said in the same language. "I will not." She fought with the thug, and then held the red stone before a torch, not comprehending why she did such a thing.

A beam of light shot out and hit the man in the forehead. He fell forward.

Then she was back in the small home which she and her son shared with Owen's mother and his brothers.

"Owen," she gasped and clutched her son to her.

"Who, Mama?" asked the little boy.

"Owen is the man for whom you are named. He is alive." She knew that Owen had survived, and that he still had the strange stone.

The stone had communicated with her. She couldn't imagine why she knew this. She did not understand it, but was unwavering in the certainty of her feelings.

Martha, dumbfounded, felt the most extreme emotions flood over her. She went from joy to despair to fear to peace. "What do I do?" she said aloud.

At that moment someone knocked on the front door to the cottage. Martha rose, trying to calm her heart. She crossed to the door and opened it.

The man who stood there recognized her at once. His face broke into a wide grin. "Martha," he cried, overjoyed.

She also knew his face at once, but she was so taken aback to see him that it took a few seconds to respond. Then she giggled with delight and threw her arms around the man. "Sholem," she laughed.

"Martha," said the man, returning her embrace. "I found you. I can hardly believe my eyes. Are you, all right?"

"Yes," she said. "Oh, yes. The staff is here, as I promised."

"Wonderful," he said. "And the stone is safe with Owen."

"It is true then," she said.

"What?" he asked.

"We heard that the British Navy hanged you and Owen with Gordon," Martha said. "But I dreamed of Owen last night. And here you are."

"Owen is alive, or was so when I saw him last," Sholem said, and grasped her hand between his. "But we were both captured more than five years ago and sold into slavery in North Africa."

"Slavery!" gasped Martha. Her right hand swept to her mouth. All these years Owen had been a slave deep in the desert.

Sholem told his story to the family that night. When he reached the part about his escape, he said with a smile, "So, I hid in the bulrushes. Not unlike my ancestor Moses."

"I know the story of Moses," young John piped. "Momma read it to me. Moses' momma made a little boat and hid him in bulrushes."

Sholem turned to Martha, who saw his delight. "You have learned to read, Martha?"

"Yes," Martha blushed. "Grace taught me," she said, taking the hand of her dear friend Mrs. McClelland.

✳✳✳✳✳

The family welcomed Sholem into their home. With his carpentry skills, he had no difficulty gaining employment on the docks. He took delight in teaching young John to read and do mathematics. At night his stories of his years in slavery and his escape from captivity, as well as his expert telling of Bible stories, made him a welcome guest in the McClelland home.

Martha wrote a letter to her uncle in England. A few months later he welcomed her aboard a sturdy ocean- going yacht. John and Sholem went aboard with her.

"Why is she going to sea? Is she going to try and find Owen?" asked Luke.

"Oh, I hope so," added Macey. *"But how would she ever find him?"*

"Well, I guess we shall have to see, won't we?" replied Mara as she continued to weave her tale of adventure.

CHAPTER TEN

Deep in the desert, Owen settled into a routine of study, work, and sleep. The household of the sheik thrived under his leadership.

One night, Owen served the evening meal to the master. He bowed and began to leave, but the master stopped him with a gesture.

"Owen," said the sheik. He indicated a cushion opposite him.

"Sir," said Owen, sitting on the cushion.

"Have you ever been in love?"

Owen hesitated, puzzled by the personal question.

"I thought so once."

"What happened?"

"I learned that the woman was married. Then her husband died, but I was too far away to return to her. I imagine she has re-married by now." His stomach tightened with pain at the thought of Martha with another man.

The sheik clucked his tongue and sat back, deep in thought. "Your father did not find another girl for you?" He took a sip of water and handed Owen a fig.

"No," said Owen, struggling not to betray his amusement. "My father died when I was young, right after the birth of my youngest brother." He bit a little of the fig and thanked the sheik.

"How old were you when your father died?"

"Sixteen. I became the sole support of my mother and brothers."

"Was this girl wealthy?"

"Oh yes. She had a pirate's treasure," Owen told him. "May I know why you ask?"

The old sheik's eyes lit up but not with greed, more like intense interest. "Tell me the story," he said. To Owen's great surprise, the sheik invited him to eat some of the meat at the table.

While Owen talked, the old sheik listened with rapt attention. As the days went by, the old sheik wrote the story down, noting names of people, locations and so forth.

#####

One morning, Owen was supervising the slaves in their work and giving out the daily assignments. The master summoned him to his tent. Owen walked in to find two sunburned white men standing before the sheik. The master gave evidence of great distress. Tears stood in the old man's eyes and his lips trembled. "Owen," said the sheik. "Go with these men. They have purchased you."

When he recovered from the shock of the news enough to speak, Owen said, "But, Master—"

"No," said the old Sheik. "I have prospered because of you. I cannot bring myself to forbid your release."

One of the men spoke to him in English. His tone was gentle and kind. "Come, lad. You are free and safe now. We have many miles to go before night and we must be off. Do you have belongings?"

It had been so long since Owen had heard English that he had to translate the words in his mind for a few moments. "I have only two things to take." He touched the stone in his pocket and then went to his sleeping mat and retrieved his *Tanach*.

The men had a horse waiting for him outside the sheik's tent. Owen begged the men to wait for a brief moment. He returned to the tent of the old sheik and found the man still weeping. "Owen," said the sheik.

Owen withdrew his glass and held it to the light. The red glow surrounded Owen with a warm peace and comfort. He took the outstretched hands of the old Sheik and the glow enveloped both men.

After a few moments, Owen covered the glass. The sheik embraced him and kissed him on each cheek. "Go with God, boy. I shall miss you."

Owen returned the embrace. With a similar blessing he left the tent. The men helped him onto the horse and they rode toward the sea.

When they had ridden out of sight of the oasis, he asked the men for their names. "My name is Lawrence," said the tall blond man. "This is Fillmore." Owen shook their hands. "A woman has been looking for you. She has spent considerable money to locate and purchase you."

"Who is she?" he asked, dumbfounded.

"We have not met her. Her uncle, whose name is Stott, hired us to find you. He seemed to know where you were. I do not know how."

Owen, baffled, couldn't remember ever meeting someone named Stott.

They rode late into the night and camped at a small oasis in the desert. Late the next day they came to the Nile River.

Within a week he arrived at the Mediterranean. The two men took him to a salon where he bathed, shaved and was given clean fresh clothing. A rowboat waited at the pier, and two men rowed him out to a large, sea worthy yacht.

"Welcome aboard, lad," said the captain as Owen stepped onto the deck. "My name is Isaiah Stott."

Owen saluted the man and shook his hand. "How do you do, sir?"

"Come. I have someone who will want to see you at once." Stott turned and walked to the back of the ship. Owen had to jog to keep up.

His heart pounding, Owen climbed down a ladder to the main cabin of the yacht. Stott knocked and a female voice said, "Come in."

Stott winked at Owen and placed him to the side of the door. He made a motion for him to stay back and opened the door.

"I have someone who wishes to see you, Niece." He beckoned to Owen.

Owen walked into the room. A tall, poised woman rose to her feet with her arm around the shoulders of a young boy to whom she had been reading. She put her hands to her mouth with a little cry and ran to his arms.

"Martha," he said, too overjoyed to speak well.

"Yes," she said, drawing back a little and indicating the boy. "This is my son John. His middle name is Owen." The boy crossed the room to him and held out a small hand. Owen took the boy's hand, noticing that the boy had deep green eyes and copper red hair.

"How do you do, Sir?" said the boy, giving his namesake, the man for whom he was named, a good grip.

"Uncle," said Martha. "Will you please take John on deck with you for a few moments?"

The boy stood looking up at Owen. He spoke in a calm firm

voice. "Uncle, I will come to you in a moment."

"Very well, John." Stott grinned at Owen. He squeezed Owen's shoulder in encouragement and left.

The boy again took the right hand of the emaciated, frightened man before him. "You are scared, Sir," said the boy. "You have been scared for a long time."

Owen felt tears start. Young John's compassion touched him to the depths of his soul. "Yes," he explained. "I have been a slave for many years."

The boy squeezed his hand and looked into Owen's eyes. Owen couldn't look away from the compelling deep green eyes of the boy. Peace and joy spilled over him.

Owen hadn't cried in several years. Now tears fell as he realized that his capacity to feel love and grace had not departed, burned out of him for good. Someone embraced him.

"Are you all right, sir?" asked the boy.

Owen wiped his eyes. "Yes, John. I have not felt this well in many years. Since the last time I saw your mother, I believe."

The boy smiled at Owen and left to join his great- uncle on deck.

"Martha," Owen said. She came to his arms and they embraced. Martha let him cry, speaking soothing, gentle words to him. In a moment they both leaned back.

Owen kissed her and gently stroked her face. "Let me look at you. I have dreamt of this face so many nights." She returned the kiss with love and reassurance. "You came for me," he said, embracing her. "You came from America to save me."

"Yes," she said. "I would have come for you sooner, but I learned that you were still alive less than a year ago." She stepped to a small table, opened the cabin door and rang a bell.

"We heard that Gordon had been defeated and killed, and that all his men had been killed or hanged. We thought you were part of them."

"You mean my mother and my family believed that I had died?" he asked.

Martha nodded. "I didn't tell her that I had found you," she said. "I needed to be sure we would be able to find you and bring you back home. To give her false hope would have been cruel. Your return will be a thrilling surprise to our community."

A man knocked and entered. Owen gaped. "Sholem," he cried. "Can it be you?"

"Yes, Owen," said Sholem Levin. The two men shook hands, then embraced, pounding one another on the back, laughing with joy.

Sholem sketched out his escape from slavery and how he found Martha. She had become determined to find him and bring him home. "About a month ago young John said he knew where you were," said Sholem. "We came. Captain Stott went ashore. He hired Lawrence and Fillmore to go into the desert in search of you. They've been gone about two weeks."

The three friends chatted for some time, catching up on years of separation. After about an hour Martha turned and smiled at Levin, who saw the meaning of that smile: Martha wanted to be alone with Owen.

"Oh yes," he said. "Yes, of course. Excuse me, Owen, we will talk later." He left and shut the door.

"We have only a little time," said Martha. "John does not like to be out of my sight very long."

"Martha," Owen said, still amazed, feeling this must be a very pleasant dream. "You came to look for me?"

"Yes. With Gordon's death, then Sholem's arrival, I no longer felt bound by my promise to Gordon. I spent a great deal of the treasure to buy this yacht and look for you."

"How did you know where to look for me?"

She gave him a strange smile, her brow creased. "I dreamed of you in the desert. Someone had tried to take the red stone. The message was very clear."

Owen remembered the night the Stone delivered him from Ashan's clutches. He rose and crossed to her. He knelt before her and took Martha's hands. "I have thought about you for years. I am," he said with complete sincerity and honesty, "and will be forever, your servant to command as you wish."

Martha, her cheeks wet with tears of joy, smiled. "Very well," she said. "I now give you your first command." She sent for Sholem to come to her cabin and perform the marriage ceremony.

Sholem, overcome with joy, married Owen and Martha that evening. That night for the first time, Owen held his new wife, afraid that if he slept, she might vanish.

The next morning Martha told him all about her life with Grace, and his brothers and sister. "They will be so glad to see you," she said. "As I was."

Something had been of concern to him since the previous afternoon. "Your son," he said. "He did something to me yesterday."

"Ah, yes, his special gift. He does it to me on occasion."

"What can he do with this gift?"

"I do not know the extent of his ability. My grandmother had red hair and emerald green eyes like his. Being around my grandmother comforted me."

"But he seemed to be able to see into my mind."

"I know," she said. "My grandmother used the word 'Cymreig'."

"I see."

"Were you frightened?"

"Of course not. The boy is gentle, kind and loving."

"Yes, he is. But many children are afraid of him in Portsmouth."

They turned the conversation to Owen's slavery and his life since she had last seen him on the bleak rock called White Island.

*****

The ocean crossing to America took several days. At last, the yacht stood off of White Island.

Martha held Owen's left hand while his new son grasped his right hand. "We must come back here after we see your family," she said.

"I understand," he agreed.

Owen's homecoming overjoyed the community of Portsmouth. His family wept with joy at his return. His mother couldn't stop smiling, thrilled that her son was safe and alive, and that her beloved young friend Martha had become her new daughter-in-law.

A week later Owen and Martha took Sholem back to what was left of Martha's cottage prison on White Island. The three worked together to hide what was left of the treasure.

Owen's knowledge of the Hebrew canon amazed the pastor of their church in Portsmouth. The young man had a fine grasp of the Hebrew language. Though he was weak in speaking the language, he had far more than an expert understanding of the written language. The pastor was astonished that Owen had memorized and translated great portions of the Old Testament.

One day, the pastor told Owen that he had written a letter to the chancellor of Harvard College. In the letter, the pastor explained that Owen was fluent in Hebrew and Arabic and had reading knowledge of Latin as well as Greek. The chancellor wrote to invite Owen to come to Boston. Owen and Martha traveled to Boston and found a small house.

Two months later Owen McClelland entered Harvard College in Boston where he studied in the Seminary for several years. He graduated and the church ordained him. He taught Old Testament Theology at Harvard for years. When he was old enough, Young John, Owen's adopted son, enrolled at Harvard.

Despite the joy in his life, and the stimulation of his studies, the horror of slavery was a long time departing from his soul. Even in the arms of his wife, he would find his thoughts and dreams haunted by memories of terror and forced labor and hunger.

In 1735 Owen buried his beloved wife on Star Island. His lifelong friend Sholem stood at his side, sharing his grief, his arm around Owen's shoulders. The treasure of Sandy Gordon passed into legend.

Sometime later, another legend was born. People recounted seeing a young woman standing on White Island, looking off to sea, as if watching a ship sailing off into the distance. The people whispered the legend of the Ghost of White Island.

PART III

CHAPTER ELEVEN

Toby and Macey stared for a while into the campfire. The story of Owen and Martha moved both of them, with the amazing power of love that the story demonstrated.

"Do people love that deeply? I mean, really?" asked Macey.

"I think, Owen knew that Martha loved him," said Luke. "Somehow that first kiss, completely changed their lives."

"Both of them, yes," said Macey, "But I have to think it really was something about the stone. After all, it wasn't until it glowed over them that they felt they belonged together."

Something occurred to Macey. "Mara," she stammered. "Were you there?"

Their Angel friend smiled. "Yes, beloved," she said. "I helped protect them, and kept them from being destroyed by fear and loneliness. But their story can serve as examples of life lessons for us to learn."

"Life lessons?" said Luke. "What do you mean?"

The Angel smiled. "In a year or so, you'll start reading and studying the plays of William Shakespeare. You'll probably read *Julius Caesar*, *Macbeth*, and maybe *a Midsummer Night's Dream*. When you are seniors, I suspect you'll read *Hamlet*. In that play, one of the characters, who's named Polonius, is schooling his son. The son is leaving his home in Denmark to study in England. He says a lot, but one thing is this quote:

"Those friends thou hast, and their adoption tried, Grapple them unto thy soul with hoops of steel, But do not dull thy palm with entertainment of each new-hatched, unfledged comrade."

Luke and Macey spent a few moments thinking about the lines from *Hamlet*. "Does that mean that you need to make good friends?" asked Macey.

Yes," said Mara. "But not just that."

"It also means to hold on to your friends and to be careful about how you select your friends," said Luke.

"That is exactly right, Luke," agreed Mara.

"Moving to a new area and a new school doesn't exactly help with that," Macey pointed out.

"Well, we'd never met before," said Luke, "but I feel like we are good friends even though we haven't known each other very long."

"An interesting comment," said the Angel. "A shared dramatic experience can bring people closer together and you two began relying on one another the moment you found yourselves transported into that ocean with no one else around."

Macey thought about what Mara and Luke said. "I guess I would agree that makes sense. If anyone asked me if I had any friends I would certainly include you, Luke," she said with confidence.

"Yeah," agreed Luke. "Me too."

"Let me give you one other piece of advice from *Hamlet*," said the Angel.

Macey and Luke glanced at each other. Mara placed her hands on their shoulders and said:

This above all: to thine own self be true, And it must follow, as the night the day, Thou canst not then be false to any man.

"I will see you again, Beloved," said their Angel friend. "Now, step through your pendants to return to Blizzard Beach." Then, as if someone had thrown a switch, Mara vanished.

CHAPTER TWELVE

Macey and Luke stood on White Island, staring at the place where Mara had stood.

"So, we're not going to say goodbye, really, huh?" said Luke.

"Yeah, I guess not," said Macey. "But I don't have any place to write down how to contact you."

"Neither do I," he said. "I think I can remember your hometown, and your high school, though."

"When we get back, I'll write them down," said Macey.

"Okay," he said. "I live in—"

But then there was a whooshing sound, and before Macey could grab at Luke, he disappeared. In the next second, White Island also disappeared, and Macey found herself next on the pool deck at Blizzard Beach.

She was deep in thought about how she would get in touch with Luke since she was whisked away so quickly when she heard her mom's voice.

"Oh, there you are." Macey turned and saw her mother, waving at her.

"What do you mean?" asked Macey.

"I've been looking for you," said Mom. "Your dad wants you to meet some of his friends from work. They have a couple of kids and I think one is about your age."

Mom had turned and was hurrying over to where their towels and beach paraphernalia were lying. Macey caught up to her, and was about to speak, when Mom looked at her more closely.

"Where did you get that outfit?" she asked, puzzled. "I don't remember seeing it before."

Macey looked down. "Oh boy," she thought. She realized that she was still wearing the outfit that Mara had given her, the one that kind of looked like a warm- up suit.

"Oh." I can't lie, she thought. Not after hearing about Martha and Owen. Their story was all about truth. "An angel gave it to me."

"What?" said Mom. Macey did her best to laugh it off, and Mom relaxed, figuring her daughter had just tucked the clothing in her swim bag.

They walked over to where their stuff was stored, and Dad came over and took her by the elbow.

"Come here, Sweetheart," he said. "I want you to meet some friends."

Macey put on a nice smile and followed her Dad to where a couple and their two kids sat, watching the activity in the pool. "Scott, Janet," he said. "Let me introduce my daughter Macey."

The couple greeted Macey and asked her to sit down. "Macey," said Scott, and he put his hand on the shoulder of a young man sitting facing away from her. The young man turned. "I want you to meet—"

"Luke!" she almost screamed.

"Hi, Macey," Luke said.

"You two know each other already?" asked Macey's dad.

"You could say that," said Luke, and the two just smirked, eyeing each other.

"Yes," said Macey. "We've had a couple of experiences together."

The two sets of parents looked at each other, confused by the comment. Luke's dad cleared his throat, "Well, you must have met earlier on one of those water slides. I'm glad Luke found a friend his age."

Macey's mom added, "Yes, Macey hasn't had anyone her age either. I'm afraid that it's been a little difficult since we moved, away from all her friends and the new school year hasn't started yet. Fortunately, we still have a couple days here at Disney."

Both teenagers began to laugh. "In that case," announced Luke, "how about if Macey and I go back to our rooms to change and then go over to one of the parks for the rest of the day and the evening?"

"Oh, yes, please," begged Macey. "That would be so much fun. But where are you guys staying?"

"Port Orleans French Quarter," he replied.

"Oh my gosh, are you kidding? That's where we are, too!"

Their parents all nodded in agreement. "Just be back before the buses stop running," one of them shouted as the two took off, sprinting for the bus back to their resort.

"I have an idea. Let's catch the bus to Disney Springs and then hop on one of the boats to take us back to the resort," suggested Macy.

"Sounds good to me," agreed Luke. "And I have an even better idea. After we each change clothes, let's meet at the cafeteria, the Sassagoula Floatworks & Food Factory, for some of those French beignets rolled in all that powdered sugar. You know, a little energy snack before heading to the park."

Macey laughed. "Those have become my favorite, too. You've got a deal."

Once they docked at French Quarter, they each hustled to their respective rooms to change. Luke beat Macey to the food court and put in a double order for the beignets. By the time she arrived he had just picked them up and taken a seat.

"I am really going to miss these once we return home," moaned Macey, as she wolfed her snack, swiping powdered sugar from her face.

"Yea, me, too. But just think of the great memories we have. Best of all, I got to meet my new friend and have the adventure of a lifetime with her," Luke said with a wink of his eye.

"I know," said Macey, "do you think we would have met if it wasn't for these pendants? How do you suppose we were chosen to hear the story of White Island and to actually be transported there?"

Luke thought hard before responding, "I think we were meant to become friends and for some reason we each needed to hear and understand the message in the story we were told."

"Sort of like Martha and Sholem," exclaimed Macey. "It really was a representation of true friendship and I know I needed to see that. I have been so upset about leaving old friends and having to make new friends that I never even wanted to look for opportunities since I learned we had to move. I have just dwelled on what I am missing instead of looking forward to starting fresh in high school. I'm beginning to think there aren't many people today that really understand friendship. After hearing about Owen, Sholem, and Martha it made me realize that some of the people I thought were good friends, really aren't."

"I am sure you are right about that and I don't think we will ever forget this whole experience," agreed Luke. "So, new friend, what park do you want to go to? You have a park hopper, right?"

"Well, have you seen the Fantasmic show at Hollywood Studios? And, yes, I do have a park hopper. We could see the 7 pm show after we do a couple rides and have something to eat. Are you on the meal plan?"

"Sounds great. And yes, I am on the meal plan."

On the bus ride over, Luke was able to get a FastPass for Toy Story Mania and Rock 'n' Roller Coaster.

Entering the park, they rushed over to the roller coaster. After screaming and laughing through the whole ride, they exited full of excitement. "Did you know that thing went upside down?" accused Macey, punching him in the arm.

Luke laughed. "You loved it. Hey, we have to get over to Toy Story pretty quick. You should like it. It's pretty tame in comparison."

"I know I will. It is my favorite ride in this park. And I guarantee my score will be much better than yours," challenged Macey as she took off running.

As they sauntered off the ride, Luke commented, "You must have had a rigged gun. No way you got that score!"

Macey just giggled. "Do we have time to hit The Great Movie Ride before we eat? It looks like there is no wait."

They both loved seeing the movies they had heard their parents talk about over the years that were featured on this ride. And they had even seen some of them. Their favorite was 'Alien', which caused them both to scream and jump. "I think I am a going to have to search out that movie when I get home," decided Luke.

They wanted to eat at Prime Time Cafe but discovered that they would never make the Fantasmic light show in time so they settled for some favorites at Min and Bill's Dockside Diner.

Luke ordered the loaded chili cheese nachos while Macey had the Carolina foot long hot dog. They both had frozen lemonade, which they finished while walking to the light show.

The crowd was fun and everyone participated in 'the wave' while waiting for the show to begin. As it ended, Macey wondered, "how in the world do they get those projections to appear so clearly on water? That was amazing. I could watch that every night."

"Very fun," Luke agreed. "Now let's catch the Star Wars fireworks show before we leave. I think it is my favorite of all the parks." They wove their way through the crowd to get a good viewing spot and were not disappointed by the spectacular fireworks and the Star Wars music that accompanied it.

On the way out of the park they had to skirt the crowds but still managed to stop and grab a giant turtle candy to share on the bus ride home. They arrived back at their resort very tired, but happy.

As they got off the bus Luke said, "I know you get to stay another day or two, Macey, but I have to leave tomorrow. I sure wish we had met earlier in the week".

"That's ok. Because of you, I am actually looking forward to this year at my new school. Thanks for a fun time today, Luke," said Macey. "I hope we will be friends for a long time even though we live so far apart."

"I am sure we will," agreed Luke. "After all we both have our IPhones and we can connect on social media, right?"

"You can count on it," she said.

~THE END~

Title: ACID

- Author: Jeff Lovell
- Publisher: TotalRecall Publications, Inc.
- HARD COVER ISBN: 978-1-59095-116-3
- PAPERBACK, ISBN: 978-1-59095-117-0
- EBOOK, Nook, Kindle, ISBN: 978-1-59095-118-7
- Number of pages: 352
- Publication Date: 2013

Rick Howell, living in the shadow of two women who have the power to change reality, must risk his life to stop the genocidal exploits of a desperate lunatic who wants to acquire their powers. The discovery of a mind controlling drug opens a pathway to frightening mental abilities for Rachel Farrell, who can move backward and forward in time at will, while Donna Riske, Rachel's best friend, can control the thoughts of others.

Title: The Coven of the Spring

- Author: Jeff Lovell
- Publisher: TotalRecall Publications, Inc.
- HARD COVER ISBN: 978-1-59095-113-2
- PAPERBACK, ISBN: 978-1-59095-114-9
- EBOOK, Nook, Kindle, ISBN: 978-1-59095-115-6
- Number of pages: 336
- Publication Date: 2013

An ancient secret, with frightening new powers, emerges to terrify and destroy.

Grace DeRosa, a gifted research chemist, lives with her husband Jim and their seventeen year old daughter Crissy. Grace finds a hidden spring in the woods near Salem, Massachusetts. She discovers that the consumed water imparts unique and fearful powers that lead to the ability to read minds, create terrifying mental pictures and force the user's will on others.

Title: Emerald

- Author: Jeff Lovell
- Publisher: TotalRecall Publications, Inc.
- HARD COVER ISBN: 9781590950807
- PAPERBACK, ISBN: 9781590950814
- EBOOK, ISBN: 9781590950821
- Number of pages: 348
- Publication Date: 2015

Emerald begins with a pirate assault on a merchant vessel. Blackbeard, or Edward Teach, terrorized the east coast of America from Nova Scotia down to the Virgin Islands. This book shows how people with a unique mental power called the Knack fight against the evil of pirates from 1715 to the present day, and even includes a long look at the court of King Arthur, and his chief advisor Myrthynne, who also had the most powerful manifestation of the Knack. This book, then, flows in several time periods and pulls together romance, villainy and a dramatic treasure, all of which frame a love story between a woman with the Knack and a man devoted to loving and protecting her.

Title: The Cape

- Author: Jeff Lovell
- Publisher: TotalRecall Publications, Inc.
- HARD COVER, ISBN: 9781590952078
- PAPERBACK, ISBN: 9781590952085
- EBOOK, ISBN: 9781590952092
- Number of pages: 228
- Publication Date: 2016

People say that *Der Fleigen Hollander—The Flying Dutchman*, as it is known in English—vanished with all hands in the sixteenth century off the Cape of Good Hope. Yet the ship has been by reliable, truthful people all over the world, suggesting that the ship is trapped in a time warp somewhere in the treacherous ocean south of the Cape. When her father is kidnapped by the ship, Therese goes to find him and rescue him from the self-imposed, Purgatorial imprisonment. In the search she is joined by her mother and a lifetime best friend, who seek to help Therese draw his soul back from the pit of Hell before he is lost for all eternity.

Title: The Ghost Of White Island

- Author: Jeff Lovell
- Publisher: TotalRecall Publications, Inc.
- HARD COVER ISBN: 9781590951194
- PAPERBACK, ISBN: 9781590952092
- EBOOK, Nook, Kindle, ISBN: 9781590952092
- Number of pages: 348
- Publication Date: 2015

In 1715, a ship's carpenter tried to rape the 14-year-old daughter of the captain of a British warship and was flogged almost to death. He mutinied and captured the ship, killing the captain and forcing his daughter into marriage. After falling in with Blackbeard, he abandoned his young wife on a cold, bitter rock called White Island, off the coast of New Hampshire. When he was caught and hanged by the British Navy, his treasure vanished into history. Many people believe that Martha, his reluctant wife, hid the treasure in the Isle of Shoals chain. This is the story of a search for those gold and jewels and treasure, protected by the Ghost of White Island.

Title: The Third Day

- Author: Jeff Lovell
- Publisher: TotalRecall Publications, Inc.
- HARD COVER ISBN: 9781590959947
- PAPERBACK, ISBN: 9781590959954
- EBOOK, Nook, Kindle, ISBN: 9781590959961
- Number of pages: 288
- Publication Date: 2016

The Old, old man walks in all the countries of the world, tracing and retracing and tracing again his betrayal, unable to find peace or grace since his betrayal of the Nazarene some two thousand years ago. Two newlywed young people and their spouses find themselves called to help him and recover an incalculably valuable treasure, worth far more than any earthly price. The group must go to the Virgin Islands and recover the treasure to help the Old Man redeem his soul and save others from a disastrous fate at the hands of a desperate cult.

Title: Jazz and Ella

- Author: Jeff & Jacqi Lovell
- Publisher: TotalRecall Publications, Inc.
- PAPERBACK, ISBN: 9781590953006
- EBOOK, ISBN: 9781590953013
- Number of pages: 104
- Publication Date: 2015

Jazz and Ella tells the story of Jazz, a fourteen-year-old high school freshman, and his best friend, Ella, who meet on the way to Disney World. A supernatural being gives them each a magic amulet, which the children use to transport themselves to new and different worlds. They meet and deal many situations that cause them to face their fears and even terrors; that suggest ways that situations can be handled; and they see some of the choices that they will have to confront as they grow up.

Title: Gina and Colby

- Author: Jeff & Jacqi Lovell
- Publisher: TotalRecall Publications, Inc.
- PAPERBACK, ISBN: 9781590953259
- EBOOK, ISBN: 9781590953266
- Number of pages: 136
- Publication Date: 2016

A Magic Amulet Allows Two Teen-Agers to Discover how to Make a Difference in the World of Animal Poaching Two teen-agers, different in every way, form an unshakeable friendship as a result of the adventures they share after meeting in Disney Springs. Transported through a magic amulet to a totally different culture and continent, they are offered an opportunity to make a difference in the lives of endangered animals.

Dangers abound as they face poachers and pirates in their attempts to rescue these creatures, and they discover a courage within themselves that leads each one to a positive change in how they view themselves and others.

Title: Marina and Dan

- Author: Jeff & JacqiLovell
- Publisher: TotalRecall Publications, Inc.
- PAPERBACK, ISBN: 978-1-59095-081-4
- EBOOK, Nook, Kindle, ISBN: 978-1-59095-082-1
- Number of pages: 128
- Publication Date: 2016

This ancient Egyptian Adventure, part of the Mouse Gate Series, traces the story of Marina and Dan, best friends since childhood, as they wrestle with the concept of heroism and how it applies to them. When offered a unique, but potentially dangerous opportunity by a spiritual being, they must make a decision that will stretch them in ways they never imagined. Able to experience first-hand the miraculous events that have been talked about for centuries, they witness the impossible become possible as they walk with Moses during the ancient biblical era where the crossing of the Red Sea took place. Both their friendship and their faith is strengthened through the adventures encountered together.

Title: *Max and McKenzie*

- Author: Jeff & Jacqi Lovell
- Publisher: TotalRecall Publications, Inc.
- PAPERBACK, ISBN: 9781590953334
- EBOOK, Nook, Kindle, ISBN: 9781590953341
- Number of pages: 150
- Publication Date: 2016

Max and McKenzie, teenaged twin brother and sister, receive magic amulets which allow them to time-travel to sites in ancient Israel. They witness Elijah's defeat of the prophets of Baal, and journey to the ancient temple of Solomon to assist in the removal of the temple treasures before the invasion of the forces of Egypt. They witness the theft of the Ark of the Covenant and its return to Israel by the Philistine forces, and march around the city of Jericho with the Israeli forces. In the climactic scene, they explore the Mount of Calvary to find the lost treasures of the temple. In their treasure hunting, they learn valuable lessons about self-confidence, personal faith, and persistent courage.

Title: The Captain's Daughter – A Macey And Luke Quest

- Author: Jeff & JacqiLovell
- Publisher: TotalRecall Publications, Inc.
- PAPERBACK, ISBN: 9781590957899
- EBOOK, Nook, Kindle, ISBN: 9781590957905
- Number of pages: 128
- Publication Date: 2018

Macey discovers her dad has taken a job across the country and must leave her home and friends. In order to soften the news, her parents take her on a vacation to Walt Disney World. At Blizzard Beach, she and a boy named Luke zoom down a water slide but pop up in water hundreds of miles away in the freezing Atlantic Ocean and a long way from shore. They are able to use a pendant that magically takes them to the shore of a secluded island. There a mysterious friend introduces them to the legend of the Ghost of White Island. The teens hear the courageous story of Martha Herring, forced into marriage with a brutal pirate, and abandoned on the miserable rock. The pirate goes back to sea, leaving Martha to guard his treasure. This is a recounting of her adventures and the challenges she and the people in her life endured. It is also the story of how the bonds of strong friendships can impact our lives.

Title: Cherokee Treasure

- Author: Jeff Lovell
- Publisher: TotalRecall Publications, Inc.
- PAPERBACK, ISBN: 9781590952344
- EBOOK, Nook, Kindle, ISBN: 9781590952351
- Number of pages:
- Publication Date: 2018

When I was a little boy, a great deal of television dealt with cowboys, and a great deal of that portrayed Indians as vicious killers. One movie had the lead character talking about the Oglala Sioux: "They're the throat cutters." But some of the most heroic and brilliant generals in our country's history were Native Americans: Crazy Horse, for example. Sitting Bull. Red Cloud, to name only a few. As a child, I was too young to have a sense of justice, I suppose, but I knew that it was wrong for the White Man to take the lands which were not theirs. It was wrong to slaughter the buffalo, as well, though the species seems to be making progress to repopulate now. Maybe I will succeed and give the land back to the Indians.

Photos from our Disney Vacation Adventure

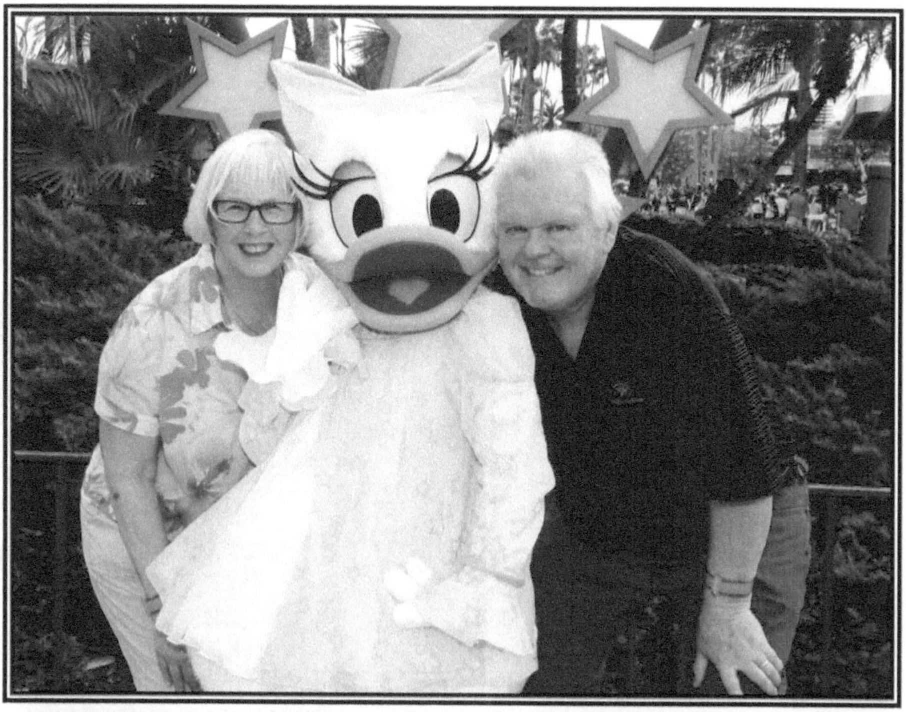

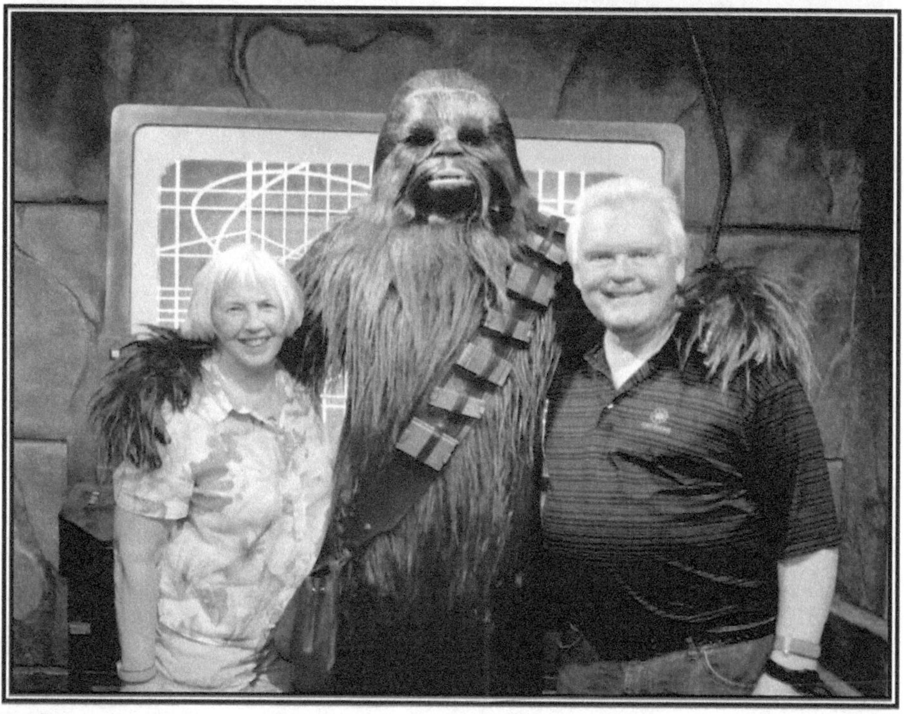

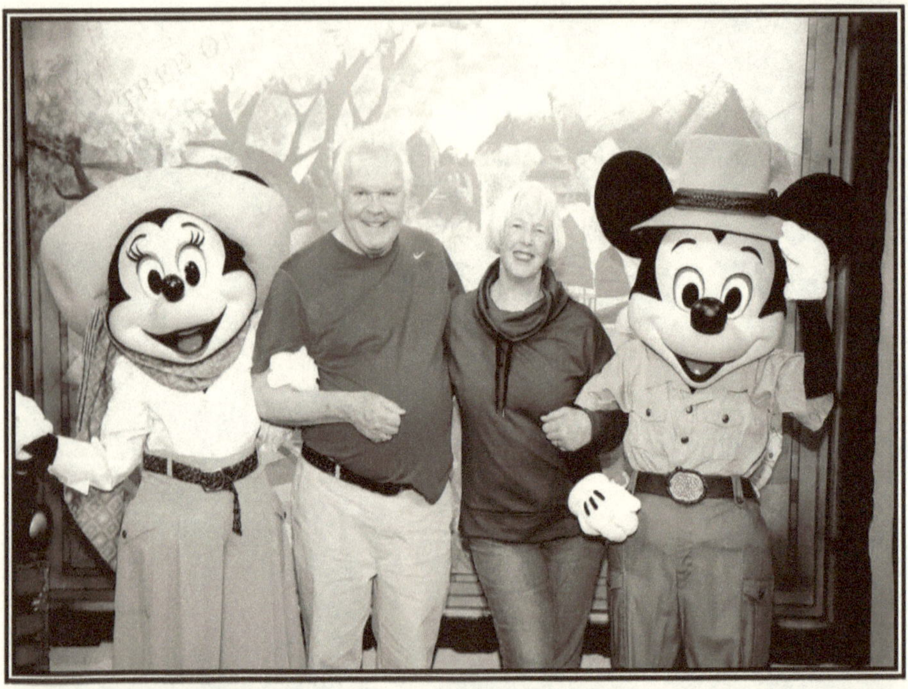

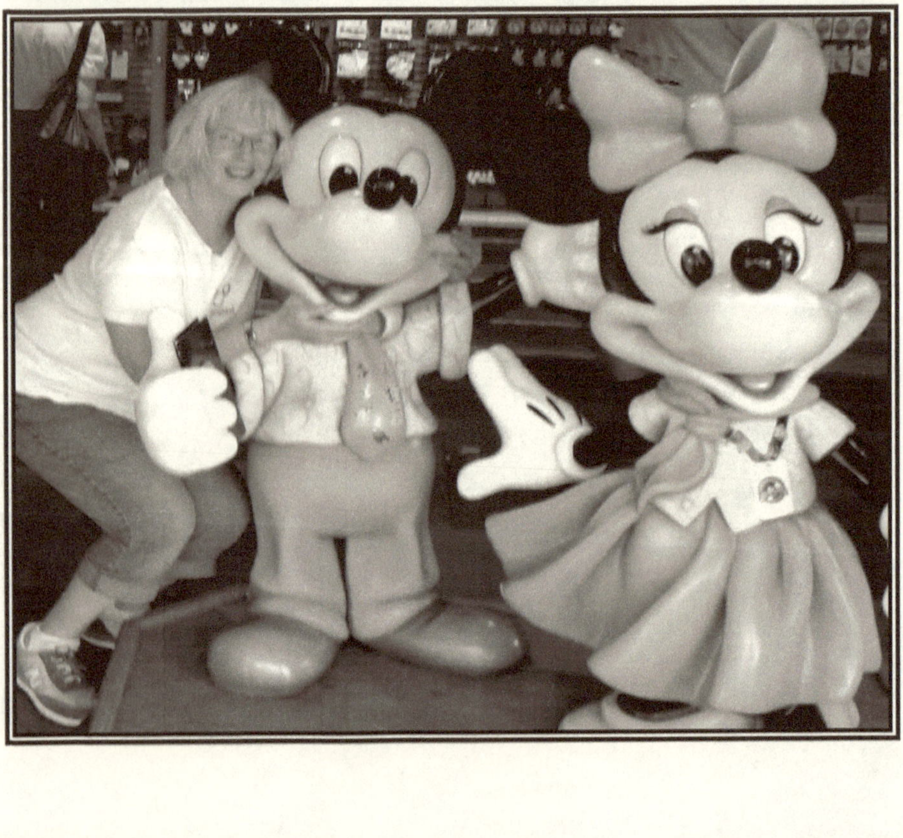

www.ingramcontent.com/pod-product-compliance
Lightning Source LLC
Chambersburg PA
CBHW020530120726
47904CB00003B/1021

9 781590 957899